SOME
EXTREMELY
BORING
DRIVES

SOME
EXTREMELY
BORING
DRIVES

STORIES

by Marguerite Pigeon

Library and Archives Canada Cataloguing in Publication
Pigeon, Marguerite, author
        Some extremely boring drives / Marguerite Pigeon.

Short stories.
Issued in print and electronic formats.
 ISBN 978-1-927063-75-0 (pbk.).--ISBN 978-1-927063-76-7 (epub).--
ISBN 978-1-927063-77-4 (mobi)
        I. Title.

PS8631.I4769S64 2014   C813'.6   C2014-901642-5
                                               C2014-901643-3

Editor for the Board: Anne Nothof
Cover and Interior Design: Justine Ma
Author Photo: Edward Pond

NeWest Press acknowledges the support of the Canada Council for the Arts, the Alberta Foundation for the Arts, and the Edmonton Arts Council for support of our publishing program. We acknowledge the financial support of the Government of Canada through the Canada Book Fund for our publishing activities.

No bison were harmed in the making of this book.
Printed and bound in Canada
First Edition: September 2014

NeWest Press

No. 201, 8540 109 Street, Edmonton, Alberta T6G 1E6
t. 780.432.9427   w. newestpress.com

In memory of Monique Pigeon, who helped me get places.

TABLE OF CONTENTS

ENDURANCE

The strangeness begins near nightfall on Day 4. Her mind's eye narrows. The regular beat of her snowshoes and the sound of her exhale, coming in short, laboured bursts, amplify. She feels calm, has the sense that she has gone inside herself, as if into a quiet room. Something takes shape in the trees, more silver than the snowy landscape, more distinct than the squalls blurring the horizon of ice. She mouths the word *robot*, but it isn't one, just an outline with a cold intention to keep pace with her, to hound her. It makes a sound like joints creaking—or are those branches? Is it wind? An oval, like a mask, pewter dull, swivels her way. It has two lights in it, pearly white and shining, snow on snow. She thinks she hears her name tickle her ear: Anick.

Panic. Her snowshoes fly, go *schwonk-schwonk, schwonk-schwonk* through the powder covering the ice, the sled bouncing behind on its tethers. Her chest burns. She huffs and snorts for air. *Stay calm*, she thinks, willing her mind's eye wider, to feel cold air against her irises, to see out and up to the vast sky. *Strange stuff always happens.* Day 2 of the Death Valley Ultra-Triathlon, Day 3 of the Race Across the Alps. *You got through those.* But she doesn't quite convince herself the same will be true this time. *I've pushed too hard. I'm in trouble. I want Michael. I want real breakfast.* This rush of thoughts takes her by surprise. Anick hates doubt. Hates pining. Despises gorging. This is her world. Right now. A frozen landscape. The race. Alaska. Four fifths of the way to the finish. She needs to remain in control. *You've hypnotized yourself is all.* It's the only logical answer. But the strange shape soldiers on at the edge of her field of vision.

She's been watching her snowshoes—the ones Michael presented her at Christmas with a stupid grin and so much reverence for their long-tailed, duckbill design. The lake ice has become brittle and feels like it could give out. To cut back to shore would've cost her too much time, so she's stayed the course, watching and calculating, her feet appearing and disappearing below. So many factors are important: time of day, indications that the powder has melted and refrozen, her own stride, on top of all her normal considerations of body temperature, position, energy level, hydration…. *I'm just dazed from thinking too much*, she concludes again. *So quit thinking.* Something worse could happen if she doesn't snap out of this. She could lose sight of what's important, of the win.

It's Michael, she complains inwardly. The thought of him 3,000 miles away, training alone for the Race Across America, the fact that she never wished him luck. *Which is his own fault!* She forces herself to break pace, closes her eyes hard and tries to slow her heart rate. She blinks them open again a moment later, pushing the frost from her lashes with her glove. Quick as that, the steely form melts between shadowed mounds of snow on shore. The strangeness passes. She changes tack, keeping her gaze firm, directed straight ahead.

Now there is only wind, metal-cold, pine-brisk air, leaden snow, the hot, regular puffs of her breath, and the darkening forest like a locked-down prison all around the lake. She feels angry, cold then hot again, and likes it: her blood's back. She falls into a rhythm and is grateful to see something else take shape across the lake. A light. Camp. *Thank fucking God*, she thinks, and shuffles the snowshoes to a more brisk beat. Schwonk-schwonk.

She unhooks her sled and pushes into the large tent with numb hands. Inside, it's not much warmer, but she flushes anyway with the temperature shift, and with relief at the sight of other human beings. A half-dozen competitors are lying around on their sleeping bags, plus support people. It's not Anick's style to seek much from her rivals, however, and the relief is overlaid, almost immediately, by hunger for rank. She might still get to teach these bastards a thing or two about endurance. *If I can keep my marbles.*

Within minutes, the warmer air brings back the pain that she has ignored all day, sets a match to her earlobes, tugs hard at her thigh muscles like at broken elastic bands. She picks up her drop, ANICK NADON written across it in block letters. It's always unpleasant to see her own handwriting and be forced back to the relative calm of the recent past, to an image of herself in her Jasper apartment, Sharpie in hand. She tears the package open and digs out a Ziploc of trail mix, stuffing a fistful into her mouth. Then she sits, wills herself to chew slowly, and pulls off her running shoes. She's too afraid of what's happened to her feet to touch her socks yet. Mac promised the new shoes would perform maximally. Now she thinks they might cost her a toe. "You can't find better," he said, bent over her feet, demonstrating optimal lace ties. "You really can't lose." Mac and his exaggerations, his twisted love of prototypes, his fancy design software, his flabby middle, his eyes already weak from years of computer-generating high-tech gear. *You mean* you *can't lose*, she thought. *Everything works perfectly in a lab*. But she didn't say so aloud. Mac, after all, has been with her since before the first big racing win, before people started lining up to pay her bills for being an elite guinea pig.

She lies back and begins her visualization of the next day's performance. She pictures her arms and legs moving easily, in harmony; imagines her breathing pushing blood into the very tips of her fingers and toes. She can almost experience the joy of finding out she's placed in the daily top three. She finishes by telling herself there will be no more seeing things, no distractions. Also, she will manage her pain.

Pain. It's all around her. Several of the competitors are having their shoulders or calves or feet rubbed by race support, which fills the tent with the smell of ointment. Anick watches them dispassionately. A room full of Solos. People like her, who don't bother with team events. It's how they get by when some races don't even pay cash prizes. More prestige, more sponsorship deals. But it's also how they like it. Anick has always hated groups, can barely handle Mac. Nearby, someone is crying and she turns to look with what is suddenly a huge effort. It's Ola, the doe-eyed Russian. Her short, damp hair is stuck to her forehead like weeds. A medic is crouched beside where she's sitting wrapped in a blanket. He checks Ola's eyes with a flashlight and shakes his head.

Ola babbles in protest, but Anick concurs: those pupils are like saucers and her cheeks are blue. *Ola's out,* thinks Anick. *She's out and her standing is toast.*

"Anick?"

She turns and flinches as her neck muscles resist the sudden movement like cold Plasticine. Last year's Men's winner is sitting on his sleeping bag two crumpled competitors away. *Reg Rogers, you egomaniac Texan creep.* "What?"

Reg gets up awkwardly and Anick notices his twin chicken collarbones. *Over-trained bastard.*

"You got extra waterproof tape?" he asks, and his voice sounds odd, like he both is and isn't addressing her in particular. Anick sees his open drop. It looks well-stocked.

"No."

Reg comes to stand over her. He reaches down towards her headband. "Your ears are burned."

Anick pulls away. "If you want to chitchat, I know a church social."

"I shit myself around hour three."

"Reg. I gotta eat."

He glares at her. The guy is fraying. Anick can tell. Reg looks confused and angry, like a child nearing a tantrum. A shadow of the guy she saw last time they met, a few months ago, at a dinner for the Endurance Runners of North America in Arkansas. While Michael was in the bathroom, Reg, all arm muscle and spring in his step, came to stand much too close, said to her, "I race because it gets me off."

"Gets you off what?"

"Don't be so butch, Anick. You're too pretty for it."

"Butch sells. Ask my sponsors." She thought then of the shot they'd chosen for the Ultra-Bar ad. She was hunched over her handlebars in a colour-block one-piece, the skin of her cheeks rippling back unnaturally against wind produced by an air machine.

"Why don't you come train at the farm? Find your softer side in the South."

"I'm good as a hardass, thanks."

"I'm sure you are—"

Michael walked back then, carrying drinks, smiling broadly. "Reg! Have a beer!" he said, offering Reg his own.

You can outrace a horse, but you can't tell when someone's trying to pick me up, Anick thought.

Tonight Reg is an X-ray of that confident player. He seems about to topple over her, but manages to plod back to his sleeping bag, where he kneels and eases himself horizontal. Anick watches him for another moment, then turns away in disgust. Sleep. The enemy, the thing she most wants, claws at the back of her eyes. She used up too much time last night, though. *Five will have to do.* She can rest come spring. And so the moment of truth arrives: gingerly, she pulls off her long "mega-breather" socks (another Mac trial).

Shit. Shit. Shit. As she's feared, early-stage frostbite has spilled like powder across both sets of toes. Her right foot is bleeding, especially the big toe. She lost the nail in her third race across the Sahara, and the toe's been left vulnerable and prone to bleeds. Right now it looks like a thick worm with the end chopped off. Carefully applying medicated cream, she recalls that event— meeting Michael there.

Night 4, she stumbled into the nine-man tent and unrolled her crinkly silver sleep sheet beside his. He turned and smiled, then went back to carefully shaking out and folding away his desert headgear. She mumbled hello, noticing something unusual in his manner. He had the familiar yellowing eyes, wind-burned skin and vine-like leg muscles of the other racers, but none of their frantic energy—none of hers. Anick has always felt that somewhere inside, something invisible squeezes her heart, generating the will—the necessary dose of fear—to go on. *What else could?* she wondered, watching him. But the longer she looked, the more untouched he seemed by the tough talk going on around them, by the posturing she was so used to. She found this irritating. *Pure tactics.* Like he could really afford to care about that filthy paisley scarf and the linen hat with its rumpled flaps.

By Night 5 in the Sahara, Anick was in serious pain from her blackening toe, nearly hypothermic from the dramatic loss of body heat after the sweltering day. The race, more grueling than she or Mac could have predicted, had forced her past the limits of her gear to the very edge of what she could endure. This was her element: endorphins made sense even of the pain, of the sand that gathered in the auricles of her ears, but they played tricks on her, too. That night, on her way to the tent, she thought she saw something rise from the desert sand. After an initial jolt of shock, she was overcome with a sense of familiarity; it was a phoenix, but not the grand mythological kind. Rather, it was the badly drawn cartoon phoenix that occasionally appeared on a show she had watched on the French channel as a kid: *G-Force: La bataille des planètes.* Ludicrous. Still, the shimmering, fiery orange wings opened a door to doubt—about her readiness, her mental capacity, her conviction that she could win solos. *G-Force,* after all, had been all about rah-rah teamwork. She'd practically bolted the rest of the way to the tent, despite her exhaustion. Around 3:00 a.m., with the desert wind howling across the open-ended tent, she started, against training and disposition, to cry. A voice nearby said, very gently, "You need rest." It was Michael. He offered to bring over his sleeping bag and lie closer to her—double the heat. Anick gulped, tasting grit, and told herself it would be a strategic advantage. They lay that way, two beaten rugs, for several hours.

Three days later, the race over (he came tenth, she seventeenth—worse than she'd counted on), they had coffee in the dusty market in Ouarzazate. He told her about his ex-wife, his job in Silicon Valley, his rock garden, his love of "World Music," his cabin in Northern Ontario. He hauled out the signposts of his life like the mayor of a town no one visited, who needed to talk up his corner of the world. The Moroccan stall owner returned over and over with more tiny, full cups.

Her shrunken stomach stretched to capacity by the trail mix, a peanut-butter sandwich and a pre-mixed vial full of vitamins, Anick zips herself, caterpillar-like, into her narrow orange sleeping bag. Mac promised her that its weave of brushed polyester microfibre couldn't fail, no matter how sweaty she became or how cold the conditions were. So far he's been right, but engineering has been beside the point; she freezes anyway—some kind of mental game she's losing. As she lies awake, shivering and damp, panic finds her again, crawls in and tingles all over. Her feet. The cold. Doubt. Pining. Michael.

Stop it. Shut up.

She blinks and the world finally goes dark, lost as though under a wave of black ink, washing away the sound of Ola's moaning.

A moment later it's morning, 4:30 a.m. She's up, headlamp on, snapping closed the high, stiff neck of her jacket, strapping on her sleigh harness. Reg brushes by her, his rear end like matched loaves of bread glazed with royal blue stretch material. He pretends she doesn't exist.

She pushes off and does three hours on the snowshoes, makes great time before sunrise. The weather is good: bitter cold, but dry and windless. Tall, narrow spruce rush past her in their green-black silence. At one point a crow startles her by flying low across her path, shining blue-black in the gauzy, heatless first light. She makes it to the juncture with the "road" (not a road at all, but not a forest or a lake or a swamp either, something like a straight stretch, and so the name has stuck among racers) at 10:17 a.m. and stops at the designated checkpoint to send in her position, praying hard. *I'll be top three. Definitely.* After a rest-up at the heated way station, she pulls her bike frame and tools from the sleigh, adjusting the tire pressure and screwing in place wheels, handlebars and seat. The bike is perfect. *You rock, Mac.* She glides down the path that was never meant for cycling, feeling eager and hungry for the next stage.

But just one hour later, fatigue lands in her lap like an anvil. She stops, dizzy with nausea, and throws up in the snow. Another racer rides up and takes in the sight, barely slowing. It's a woman. Favoured to place. French. Someone who has always bristled at Anick's regional accent and Franglish.

"*Vous appellerez si cela continue, oui?*" the woman calls flatly, as she pedals by, insectile in her covered boots and black helmet.

"*Oui, oui.*" But there's no way Anick is going to use her secure signal over a bit of puke. Just turning on her phone guarantees someone would come. She'd lose the day, never catch up. *You'd like that, wouldn't you? Maudite snob.*

The French woman nods and speeds away in a fierce display of kneecaps. Alone again, Anick pulls out her tube of espresso-flavoured energy gel and sucks the bittersweet goo. *Let's go.*

Back on the bike, struggling up an icy incline of exposed roots, her mind drifts again to Michael. It was just a week after the Sahara race when he emailed her the invitation to his cottage. *For-get it!* she said to herself, rolling her eyes with a chuckle that surprised her by sounding like genuine regret. But she couldn't go. She wasn't good with vacations and worse with men. There had been moments when she'd thought she'd been in love. One cold winter in Whistler with an Australian ski instructor. Then that bike builder in Nevada who wanted her to quit racing and go into the dog breeding business with him. It was all so exhausting, such responsibility. To her, sex was like a long break between races; after a while, you could forget it was just a pleasant waste of time. Alone, she'd been at her best, could channel her fear, win more races.

She texted Michael. Can't make it. Bk in Jasper & work's crazy. German biz types here to train. They want to sweat blood and pay me for it.

He replied immediately, but by email, a long message in which he provided a lot of details of his own work, in no rush to get to the point. Anick scanned down to the bottom. Don't think of it as downtime, he wrote. The country's ideal for trail running. And fishing. And stake eating. Think about it, anyway. A carnivore, like herself. A bad speller, too. Reading his words, she felt an inkling of the peculiar difference that she'd noticed in Michael in the desert. She weakened.

Michael turned out to be as amazed with sex as he was with everything else, eager to explore the mechanics of it all. He didn't bug her with too many questions or gush about nature. He filleted the measly pickerel she caught. Most days, he was satisfied to make love and cook elaborate breakfasts. He did tell her endurance racing made him feel "spiritual." She let out a snort and immediately regretted it, seeing his face fall. "I just didn't know it could," she said, and it was true. From the first time she put on running shoes, she's simply wanted to get as far as possible from weakness. Everything, it seems to her—her whole career—has flowed from that.

Afterwards Michael came to visit several times, making her download an interactive calendar where they could plan races to do together—The Mount Diablo, The Belle Isle Ultra—the dates cheerfully filled in with vibrant red and yellow highlight. They attended that Arkansas dinner, spent Christmas in Colorado. He gave her the snowshoes. On New Year's Eve day they tested them out, doing six hours out and back into high, fluffy snow country. But she got annoyed when he wanted to stop along the way to talk or to slide a gloved hand up the back of her jacket. She pulled ahead significantly, but slowed down again when she looked back and saw that he looked small, sadness settled on his shoulders. She stopped, kissed him, felt under his toque for a patch of bald head to rub.

But on New Year's Eve, at their cabin, the inevitable. It began when she refused some champagne he'd surprised her with. The outing had got her thinking about the Alaska race and she was worrying about her nutrition.

"Anick," he said, letting the unopened bottle sink back down into melting ice.

"Yes?"

"I have to train really hard for the Race Across America."

"So go hard!" She stuck a finger in his ear and gave it a wiggle.

"Right. Well, that's what I was considering…. Would you think about leaving Alaska until next year? I mean, we would do it together then."

Her finger stopped. A silence stretched. "Michael," she said finally, "if you want me to chase after you while you do the R.A.A., snowshoes were a dumb idea."

She stood up from the couch where she'd been lying, not sure what to do with herself.

"It's not that I don't want you racing," he said, exasperated. "It's just that I thought we could take turns: you come with me this year and I go up North with you next."

"I don't need a shadow," she said, feeling less sure about this than she let on.

It was their last night together. She tried to give back the snowshoes but he wouldn't take them. She landed back in Canada in the middle of a soupy snowstorm feeling equal parts emotional exhaustion and anticipation, could barely face the snowshoes as they dropped, bagged, tagged and dispiriting, onto the slow-moving conveyor belt. The next day, 5:00 a.m., serious training resumed.

Now it's 9:20 p.m. The northern night sky is purple ink flecked with sparkles. Anick is beyond tired, has passed over to a fuzzy state where pain, cold and damp jostle for space in her mind like ice cubes in a shaker. Her element. But the border of it, where certainty and doubt touch. She places the beam from her headlamp on the spot just ahead of her front tire. The bike, it turns out, isn't perfect. She's had to stop four times to adjust tire pressure so far. *You suck, Mac.* Her health, too, sucks: another vomiting session in the midafternoon, numbness in the toes that she can't ignore anymore. And the weather has turned windy and snowy. When she finally hit the mandatory waypoint at 7:45 p.m., the flag was gone. Probably snagged by *La Snob*. Anick spent a few precious seconds swearing and kicking snow before moving on.

Since then she's devoted herself to making up time, using a regular dose of supplements to keep up her calories. She's not prepared to do much more. She should eat another energy bar but doesn't have the energy. This old joke, plus the state of her toes and her tedious pace, all combine to make her laugh out loud, but the sound is like a raucous crow in the silence of falling snow. She hasn't seen anyone since lunchtime and suddenly she feels very alone. A longing rekindles for Michael's breakfast: bacon and eggs with slices of melon. *No more Michael!* she orders. She wants to put on another layer of clothes or switch back to the snowshoes, but can't bring herself to stop and pry open the closed-topped sleigh with her frozen hands. *Stay focused*, she thinks. *Focus.* Camp must be close. *I can still win.*

She is pushing through snow chunky enough to suggest a creek below, trying to get her bearings, when her wheels catch in some especially gummy thickness and she has to dismount to grind through to the next rise. Gloved fingers wrapped around her light, narrow handlebars, pushing hard from the thighs, she works forward in slow, deliberate steps, but gets light-headed from the effort. Nearly through, she looks up and is stunned by what she sees: a man, kneeling in the snow. His back is to her, the tails of his silver snowshoes pointing straight up, his sleigh, unhooked, off to one side. She drops her bike, unhooks her own sleigh and runs, grabbing his shoulders and turning him around.

Reg.

His face is grey. He looks at her wild-eyed, searching her face with the fervour of a child lost in a department store. His hands come up to touch her shoulders. "Uhm vehry tttired. Zts' not—camp's not herrre."

"Ok. Ssshh. It's there. Just calm down, Reg. Did you call in?" Reg babbles on, not processing her words. Anick pats his jacket for his phone or tracker, but either he's misunderstood the gesture or he still can't accept calling for help, because he pushes her away. "Don'…Don'," he says, his hand arcing forcefully across his chest to remove hers.

"You have to call in, Reg."

He laughs thinly. "Okay. Okay. Bye!" he says, clapping a glove against her chest several times. "Bye bye, baby!" The sound makes Anick's stomach drop. She remembers Michael, clapping with real gumption when she pulled her fish into the boat. It slapped the aluminum bottom—alive, fighting for air.

She tries again to unzip Reg's jacket. This time he yells, "Let me be!" and shoves her. Anick falls back into the snow, surprised and furious. *I should leave you here.* She could make her way to camp, send help from there, her check-in time unaffected. But Reg has tipped onto his side and is lying with half his face in the snow, his tongue dangling. *Fuck.* What choice does she have? She unzips her own jacket and digs for her phone, wanting to scream. But as her hand goes into the inner pocket it is always zipped into, she realizes: that last, half-squeezed energy tube; she put it back into the wrong pocket, exactly where Reg just shoved her. *Câlisse de….* Her phone, as she pulls it out, is covered in brown ooze. She has to pull back the fingers of her glove to handle it properly, and in the bitter cold it's like striking each fingertip with a match. She fumbles with her plastic case but it's no good. The goo has gotten inside. If the phone works, she can't tell because the screen is a depthless black. She uses her tracker to send out her position—she can explain her way out of a disqualification, she hopes—but she also knows a GPS position won't get as fast a response as the phone.

She turns back to Reg. He seems to be falling asleep. Anick looks around, suddenly frantic. She rushes over and clicks open the latches on his sleigh, pulling out all the clothes she can find as well as his sleeping bag. After popping off his snowshoes and yanking off his trail shoes, she tries to shove a Gore-Tex shell under his purple ass and pull him to sitting on it by grabbing both his forearms. It's a comedy of failed attempts. Reg keeps sliding down with half giggles, half moans, snow melting off his waxy face. She finally gets him upright, tugs extra socks over his frozen feet, then pushes more layers over his head. The effort further drains her, and only fear keeps him in focus—ghostly in the beam of her headlamp.

Then she inches the sleeping bag over his feet, her slow-working mind evaluating the situation. *Way worse than Ola.* Reg isn't even shivering. With much tugging and despite its narrow design, she zips herself into the bag with the Texan up to their waists, at which point she takes advantage of Reg's floppiness to pat him down again. She finds the tracker right away, but no phone. Not having it with you during any stage of the race is an automatic disqualification, a go-home-do-not-pass-go guarantee. But for a guy like Reg, Anick knows, racing is risk; he could've left it behind on purpose. She sends out their position with his tracker, doubling the chances of a response, before zipping their upper halves up to the armpits, like into a shroud. She grips Reg's whole body then, unsure how much heat she has left to give.

"You're an idiot," she says.

His chin against her shoulder, Reg drools out something that sounds like, "Wuhr tahgethr."

"It just looks that way." Anick shifts and their cheeks touch. She has an experience then, of seeing herself from above. She is sure, suddenly, that this is Michael. Here, lying beside her. Something squeezes her from the inside and claustrophobia rises like a fever from her burned toes to her numb ears and she cannot stay lying down a moment longer. She gets out and goes to her bike, pulling it up, then turning it around and hauling it, with the sleigh coasting behind, her breath an exaggerated wheeze, back to where Reg is lying. She drops the bike, gets on her knees and exposes her fingers again to work open the sleigh's frozen hinges until the top half is completely released. She chucks all of its contents—all her expensive clothes and tools and gear (she prays that she overstocked her next drop)—into the snow, leaving just the empty bowl of the sleigh bottom, which she unhooks from her bike and places lengthwise beside Reg. Then she pries Reg's side up off the ground, howling aloud with the effort, seeing spots float into her field of vision, her hands like heavy, dumb oafs she cannot communicate with. Somewhere in her mind she hears the question: *What about the win?* But the thought won't stick. She is too busy tipping Reg's weight over the lip of the sleigh, trying to slide the rest of him in, failing several times. Once, she simply collapses over him. *Fucking ridiculous.*

Finally, on her fifth try, Reg, miraculously, slips into the bowl of the sleigh, the bottom half of his sleeping bag dangling off the end like a tongue. Anick, tears freezing on her cheeks, hooks the sleigh back to the bike, pulls up her handlebars and, holding them straight, begins to push ahead, back over the roots and rocks and snow she came through just minutes ago. It is farcical, exhausting. The sound of her breath increases in volume. Fantasy and reality begin to converge as they did just before the strangeness began yesterday. She stops, widens her ears, her eyes, slaps herself in the face and screams just to shake herself awake. But this time it's her own limbs that seem to be made of rusty hinges, her own skin that is silver-cold, her face a hard oval, and inside, nothing, just that insistent squeeze, insistent against the outer shell.

"Wuhr tahgethr," says Reg, again. She wants to tell him to shut up so she can concentrate. Maybe they'll meet the search crew halfway.

She's finally getting somewhere, nearly on a welcoming flat stretch, when her foot catches what must be a tree root and she falls in such a way that the small bolt between her handlebars smacks her on the nose and blood spurts out. She tries to get up, but the snow is like muck. She is trapped, dragged down by the weight of Reg. Soaked. Fatigued to the core of her being. Her toes have begun a revolt inside her shoes. She recalls the night in the desert, the burning cartoon bird, her disgust at childhood programming that encouraged group work, the relief of Michael's offer of heat, how little pain she'd felt during those hours. She'd felt nothing, really. Like sitting in a boat on a lake when there's no wind.

Her eyes, through frozen lashes, search the trees, looking for camp, for the single penetrating light of the snowmobile eating up the snow with its treads, hurrying forward to spot them.

LOCKS

The cancer drugs stole my hair. Plucked me naked. What's grown back is like a message spelled out millimetre by millimetre: I'm not who I thought I was. A redhead. Whimsical. Someone whose nickname could be Pumpkin. The new crop, near black and coarse, is all business. Each follicle mocks me, says, "Red, schmed!" then pushes out its dark strand. I hate it even more than I hated being bald.

"I just *love* it," says my hairdresser, Li, who is always ready to lie in the name of hair. I return to her hydraulic chair after an eternity of illness without the hurrah I imagined would follow me in like a whirlwind, little bells above the door heralding Crystal Gayle, Rapunzel, Goldilocks. Reality is more subtle: piped-in adult contemporary, an enviable scatter of tufts on the floor, stubborn mirrors conspiring to show me a swollen, pallid version of my true self with two inches of the dreaded dark hair.

"I'm thinking highlights," says Li. She uses a voice like many acquaintances do now, intended not to further disrupt my brittle bones. I feel I am being spoken to from very far away. Li opens her fingers into a splay and runs them abruptly through the rough mass several times, alternating hands, like her palms are planes taking off from the crown of my head.

"Or more sophisticated," she says, reassessing, reading something in the tussle. "Back to red, maybe."

"No. Not red." I'm thinking about my husband, the first time he ever loosened the red bun I used to like to wear low on the nape like a tomato. The image gets blurred by self-pity, so I shake it away.

"Blonde," I say. "White-blonde, like snow."

Li's hands come out of my hair, pause palms down. My head could be a drum she will play. Her shocked silence lasts a long time and I feel oddly ashamed to be undergoing yet another evaluation.

"Blonde's *always* big," she finally agrees, with gumption. "It'll refresh you."

My treatment schedule resulted in my sometimes seeing the same people at the cancer centre. Like this one old woman—lungs, Stage 3—who knit incessantly. She was Estonian. So said the nurses, who all loved her positive attitude and the patterned mittens she would give out to anyone who wanted them. This woman would wheeze and wheeze while her needles went *click-click, click-click,* contentedly stitching away her life. A goddamned swan song in patterned double-knits. I would turn the volume up high on my iPod and look away, feeling rage, like boiling water, pouring through my insides. I wished I could take those knitting needles and stab the old woman's heart. Stab my nurses. Stab the tube that was feeding me poison so that the liquid exploded out. One time, when my iPod battery died and I was feeling suffocated by the needlework two chairs down, I finally snapped. "For God sakes!" I yelled at the old woman. "Will you please can it?" One nurse who'd never liked me put a finger to her lips in a violent shushing gesture. Without thinking, I flipped her the bird and laughed, even though I knew it wasn't funny. I turned to look at the old woman. She was facing resolutely away from me. Her forearms had fallen against her sides. The needles and wool webbing were plopped on her belly in a vanquished red and green pile. She sniffled a while, her shoulders heaving, then began to snore. I watched her irregular breathing, couldn't look away for the satisfaction it gave me. Mind you, I always looked to that side—away from the arm getting the drip. But still.

"You won't want me to stay just because of all that's happened. I know that much." He said this not long after I was finally home for good. I guess my husband was so used to speaking to people on my behalf, he'd begun to confuse his will with my own. We were sitting at the kitchen table, where I once pictured myself sitting for life. He'd brought home takeout Thai.

"You never liked this neighbourhood anyway," he said, trying to be lighthearted.

"I like the library."

"Hmm," he said disapprovingly. "Look, we'll wait till you've found your feet, but you won't want this to drag on forever."

"I want this to drag on forever."

He put his face in his hands and started to cry while I went on eating. All the crying of that period! It was epidemic. But the food was delicious. I liked the sweet and the spicy together. I loved the lime. The surface of things *did* matter, I thought. Taste. Touch. Appearances. The semblance of normal life was my ticket back to the world of the living. This new woman, "clean" of cancer, released from the pen of hospital and chemo, needed a husband. At any cost.

The week my hair finally began to grow back, forming a sudden shadow on my head like a map of a strange continent, my husband was in Montreal on business. I was avoiding former friends and had not seen a soul for days. One evening I was standing in my underwear in front of the bedroom mirror, trying to believe I'd lost some weight, longing for nineteenth-century illnesses that wasted people instead of fattening them, when I found myself wandering over to the closet. I stood facing my hanging clothes, most of which I hadn't worn in so long they didn't smell like me anymore but like the house, and like my husband. Everything bore his stamp now—he'd taped his hockey pool to our bedroom mirror; the bathroom cupboard was full of musky men's soap. I reached in and fondled the material of a dress, then tore it from its hanger and put it on. I crouched down, the material bunching around my middle, and tossed shoes out of the closet until I found a pair I liked. Then I dug out an ancient sequined purse, drew on lipstick—twice, in thick strokes—and called a cab.

On the way downtown, I rolled down the window and stuck my head out into the bitter night air. It nipped my nostrils like tiny metal hooks. The cabbie eyed me through his rearview.

"Just watch the road!" I sniffed, but it didn't come off. Half the words were taken from my mouth by the wind. I saw the cabbie shake his head. "Stop here," I said, when we finally reached a cluster of popular bars outside which young people were smoking and looking jaded. I paid and went into the one called Millennial Men.

Inside it was very dark except for long purple lights outlining the performance area. Frenetic electronic music. Big groups of women everywhere. A whiff of violence as I breathed in their clashing perfumes. Everyone was applauding a dancer named Risky Business, who was making his exit wearing an unbuttoned white shirt and nothing else, two long, stretched-out white tube socks slung over one shoulder, stuffed with money. I squeezed through the crowd and took a seat away from the rest but close to the stage. A waiter, whose fake tan was the colour of peanut butter, came by to take my order.

My first drink. It had fruit dangling from it. I toasted. "To melon balls!"

There was a pause before the next dancer. The lights came up. I saw how ugly the place was. All the matte-black paint on the stage and floor was scratched and gritty. I sipped my drink. The energy at a table nearby shifted and I heard whispers directed my way. I thought of my ugly noggin reflecting the mean-spirited ceiling lights. I shot the women a kill-kill look, sucked harder on my straw, and raised my hand for another.

My husband and I met at a martini bar where I felt I didn't fit in but used to go anyway. He laughed at a dirty joke he overheard me make to a friend. We danced sweatily, then went home together.

"What do you think of this?" he said one day, a few months later, when we were out for lunch near his office. He was holding out a pamphlet for a resort in Belize.

"Are we going on the lam?"

"I think we should. I think we should get married there, Pumpkin." I agreed, and we went. I didn't think much about it. We got along and neither of us had ever been given a reason to say no to new possibilities. Two years after Belize, I got pregnant. My husband was ecstatic. He'd put his cheek to my belly all the time.

"Productivity up this quarter," he'd say, refusing to bow to trimestrial accounting. When I miscarried, he was more disappointed than I was. "We'll build another factory," I told him. But we never did. I got sick for the first time just a year after that.

From the start I saw by the way my husband supported me in my illness—coming with me to appointments, cleaning up my puke after treatments, relating optimistic medical reports he'd seen on TV—that he was compensating. He was, after all, wholly strapping. After my diagnosis, his easy health and prosperity felt like overly fancy clothes. Showy. Awkward. The more he tried to hide his vigour, the more he eclipsed me—and resented me. I couldn't really blame him. Not yet.

A purple spotlight dangling on a pivot above me swung excitedly into an arc as the announcer prepared us for the arrival of the Jamaican Jiggler. A man appeared on stage to an accelerated reggae beat. Not more than twenty-three, black, oiled, narrow in the hips, and, to my mind, painfully effeminate. The women went wild. The Jiggler lived up to his name and shook his half-erect penis with enthusiasm, crouching low and barefoot. One unsteady, dishevelled bride-to-be with helium balloons tied to her big ponytail was thrust at him. She put her hands up to her eyes as if to shield herself from the sight of the naked dancer, but she was giggling like crazy. The Jiggler shimmied around her. Up and down. Circled her in faux-tribal fashion. Conducted rapid hip thrusts. She squealed and released a twenty-dollar bill into his clenched jaws.

The Jiggler sprinted into the crowd. I followed his zigzag through the tables until I lost sight of him then gave up, looked back at the stage and waited for the next act. Suddenly, from behind, two hands took me by the armpits and lifted me to my feet. Nearby, women went, "Whoo-hoo!" Unsteady, I turned to look, but the Jiggler had already released me and had come around the front, looking me in the eyes. Slowly, he leaned in and brushed my lips with his own. They were coarse and warm. Then he slid his hands up onto my bald head, over the prickly five o'clock shadow, while, below, he continued his unsettling, sexless jiggling. Above the neck I saw that he was fine-featured and soft-eyed, and I recognized things I'd assumed had been removed from my world. Generosity. Sensuousness.

Without planning to, my own fingers came up to rest over several of the Jiggler's dreadlocks. No sooner had I registered their warm, dry thickness than he pulled away, taking my hand, extending my arm and dramatically withdrawing, leaving my hand lifted, empty and trembling, while he resumed the false, devil-may-care smile that made some women near the stage jump up and down like little girls, their own big, gelled, sprayed hair swinging around sloppily.

Later, in bed, when the call came that I knew was from my husband, in Montreal, checking in as I'd pleaded with him to do, I let it ring through the empty house, then turned off my bedside lamp and fell immediately to sleep.

My eyes are closed for a long time. When I open them, Li is standing behind me.

"What do you think?"

"I'm like Susan Powter," I say. "Without the muscle mass."

Li laughs nervously. I pay and she follows me to the door, telling me she'll be happy to do a touch-up in a couple weeks. Free. Just call.

I walk outside to wait for the man who is still going through the motions of being my husband. On the street a young girl and her mother have paused nearby, talking to an acquaintance. The girl has a short bob of hair, blonde as mine and fresh as fleece. She carries a poodle that has been dyed pink. She has a bored, rich-brat demeanour and strokes the dog absently.

"Is he yours?" I ask, then scan the street both ways. My husband is late.

"*She*—yes, she's mine," says the girl. The mother, who is gesturing emphatically to her friend about something, ignores us.

"Pets are a lot of work."

"We have doggie daycare Mondays, Wednesdays, and Fridays," says the girl, shrugging her shoulders. Though she cannot be more than six years old, she checks her watch as if she has someplace better to be. For a long moment we stand there, pretending not to notice one another. Suddenly, a car horn blares nearby, making us both jump. My husband pulls quickly to the curb and waves sheepishly from the driver's seat. He is still handsome in that way that makes some women grin like fools around him.

"Is that your boyfriend?" says the girl. I can't tell whether she's really asking or just making fun of me, and I start to feel old and ungainly. A Sharon Stone impersonator. Not a trace of Pumpkin.

"Used to be," I say. At a loss, I bend over to pet her dog. I am surprised to find its fur silky, incredibly soft. Then, that pathetic pink creature rolls up its matched, milky eyes and gives me a look of such open eagerness that I don't try to shoo it. We keep close, nearly nose to nose. I can tell I've unnerved the girl, who reaches for her mother's hand and begins to withdraw. The pink poodle resists though, its warm body wriggling every which way, straining. It sticks out a small, greyish tongue and manages to lick my entire face in several wet slaps, from my chin to my new, near-white spikes. I straighten up, turn, and walk to the car, sniffling, holding my palm to where the animal's saliva is drying on my cheek.

Inside, the air conditioning is blaring away and my husband is looking down at his lap with his hands on the wheel. Something about him makes me recall the moment when I felt closest to dying, how I'd secretly yearned to get it over with. I take his right hand and put it to my hair. He startles, clearly repulsed. "See? It feels totally new," I say, ignoring this. Then, turning to wave at the little girl, who is no longer paying attention, I let it go.

SLAG

The fight starts as a joke. They're horsing around. Wrestling. She tells him he's a wuss. He calls her a ball-breaker. She hits him harder on the arm than she's intended to, and laughs because she expects him to find it funny, her being so slight. But the part of him she knows well, which is primed for conflict and can't take a joke, has been provoked. The punch lands just above her elbow with enough force that she feels his knuckles smack bone. He looks at her arm then back up at her face with a questioning half-smile. Just now he could be Lazar's son—an undeniable family resemblance Giselle has always downplayed. The smile invites her to consider her reaction, asking her what will happen next, as if it's her choice. But she can tell they've already crossed a line. Thought is a disadvantage now. She pushes him in the chest with everything she has and, when he falls backwards, starts running. He grabs her ankle and pulls it out from under her. She hits the carpet, the wind knocked out of her lungs. She is angry enough to howl, but there's nothing left to scream with. She is like those pelt rugs, the wolf mouth preserved, baring teeth, but no howl. She steels herself, kicks at his hand with the heels of her socked feet. He deflects and crawls alongside her, takes her by the shoulder, rolls her onto her back, and gets on top. The smell of soap descends from his shirt where the collar sags. Like his uncle, Gabe has always been very clean, though he would say Lazar is a dirtbag, no matter what.

They struggle and Giselle manages to push the butt of her palm into Gabe's nose. He turns away in pain. When he turns back, he has become a stranger with a lower face full of blood. For a moment he looks like he might actually laugh, might realize they've gone too far. Meanwhile, seeing the blood makes her feel good. She dislikes this good feeling. It is satisfaction. She hopes Gabe *will* laugh, that she will not want more. But he replies with a punch across her cheekbone that reminds her of exiting a warm house underdressed on a night of extreme cold. Everything tingles in the moment of shock. Then a burn spreads from her cheek to the crown of her head. She tries to push him off, but her whole body, her mind and her heart are suddenly leaden. The possibility of his weak smile, even the sweet note of revenge she has just experienced, is erased. It crosses her mind that this is when a lot of guys would try to force sex, but that isn't him. She can't say her situation is better—the fight doesn't have an obvious end. She thinks again of her mother and Lazar, how difficult it will be to hide the marks from them, but how she will have to, and how Gabe will too. Who knows how blame will come down if they find out?

They are in Gabe's room. Fifteen minutes ago, they were making out. His every touch was a salve. His body soothes her—has since she first kissed him at one of Lazar's parties. Gabe had been enough of an outsider there to stand out. He's always liked to tease and tickle her. But this time the tickling went on until Giselle's breathing became convulsive. Now, besides her own blood, she can taste the gum he was chewing. Raspberry. Probably stuck to the carpet now.

The phone rings in the hall and the sound jolts him like it's a bell ending a round of boxing. Mid-punch, he slows his fist and gets up, breathing hard. He walks out of the room, leaving the door open. From where she lies, she watches him stand by the phone, catching his breath. "Hello?" he says, sounding normal. "It's Gabriel. She isn't here right now." He picks up a pen, clicks out the ballpoint. "Can I take a message?" They are both seventeen.

A year later her mother comes home, puts down some packages and unzips her boots. "Giselle? Giselle, you there?" she calls, patting down the hall. She stops, framed in the long rectangle of hall lights, her thinness accentuated, her legs, reedy as a bird's, sheathed in leather leggings. "You don't answer?"

"What."

"Where's Gabe?"

"Midterms."

"He still doing that?"

"By 'that,' you mean university education?"

"It's not like he couldn't have a job."

"Whatever."

"*Dieu Seigneur*, you're in a mood. I bought you a sweater."

Giselle lifts her back from the couch. "Can I see?"

"Tomorrow. Laz is back early. He needs some down time tonight."

Giselle turns up the TV.

"Gis? You hear?"

"Fine."

Her mother retreats from the door. Giselle can predict her actions with confidence. Her mother will track Lazar's flight, then shower and change into one of the outfits she is forever buying. She'll turn on the oven and take some fancy hors d'oeuvres from the freezer. She will sit in her room against a stack of silk pillows and watch her enormous TV. *Real Housewives*. Or the news. The volume will be turned down low enough so that she won't miss the sound of Lazar pulling into the driveway. Then she'll rush to the kitchen to put the pastry puffs or whatever on a tray, and pour them both wine in the stupid, oversized glasses they drink from. Giselle doesn't need to be here for any of it, to see her mother regress even further from grown woman to kept hostess, or to bask in the cologne-scented, overdressed, shaved gorilla that is Lazar. She knows the deal. She packs a bag and heads to Carla's.

"Bangfest over there, eh?" says Carla, opening the door.

"Gross."

"I bet they have the hottest sex," she says, leading Giselle to her room. Carla is in her first year at the local college, training to be a dental assistant. She says that unless her tits fall off she will marry a dentist and live where all the established families live— on the clean lake that's stuck in the centre of Sudbury like the blue iris of an eye that's black everywhere else. For now she lives at home and smokes a lot of pot. As soon as she closes her bedroom door, Carla sparks up. They smoke flanked by low shelves crammed with the fat limbs and bug eyes of her old stuffed ani-mals, Carla talking about the electronic engineering student she's sleeping with, how he's too much of a dork to go down on her and how she's going to trade up soon. "Like you should move on from Gabe," Carla says, nudging her.

Giselle shakes her head hard. They rarely talk about her rela-tionship. It feels impossible.

But Carla has a hard time reining herself in once she gets go-ing on any topic. "It's just, how can you know? What's good in a guy. What's out there. Unless you try some out." She raises and lowers her eyebrows meaningfully.

Giselle frowns, thinks of the men she's known. An image forms of her father dragging himself out the door to work; then Lazar, when her mother first allowed him into their lives, his tough-guy wraparound sunglasses and angry smile; and Gabe, the small tattoo on his inner arm that says WORK HARD OR DIE. Giselle runs out of images. "That's your thing, not mine."

Carla, a self-proclaimed sex maniac, usually laughs at a good provocation. So Giselle can tell something serious is coming when her friend frowns. "I'll tell you this much," says Carla. "Next time Gabe loses his shit, you can't hide out here till you look normal. I'm outta this shithole. You remember that girl I was telling you about, in my program? Rebecca? I'm thinking of getting an apartment somewhere near school with her. She's cool. We can afford it once our placement starts." She scans Giselle's face. "What do you think?"

Carla shrugs. "Sounds great."

"You'd be able to come over anytime."

"It's far."

"Not really. You'll like it. Can you imagine how hard we can party in my own place?"

Giselle nods but can't hide her hurt.

"Are you serious right now? You're the one who didn't want to move out. Got it too good at your mom's."

"I want to save my own money."

"Call me when that happens."

Giselle shoves her in a friendly way. "So mean!"

"Truth telling, that is all. Gabe's the one who's gonna end up with cash. Admit it. That's why you don't drop him and run."

"He's going to be a refugee lawyer. Help people."

"I can totally see that. He won't be tempted at all to work for Laz and his boys. Never ever."

"Carla."

"Let's move on," says Carla. "This is killing my boner." She turns the music up, stands up on her bed and does a zealous imitation of Lady Gaga, her eyes fixed straight ahead and her substantial ass going off to one side and back. Both of them crack up.

They talk endlessly about nothing else of importance. Eventually, Carla falls asleep and Giselle watches her friend's lips moving softly in and out with her breath. She puts her arm over Carla, enjoying her softness. Some time later, she sleeps too.

The next day, Carla's father, Jean-François, starts on a drunken bender. They do what they can to avoid setting him off, but it's just a matter of time. That night they are back in Carla's room, playing their music, having a beer, getting ready to go out with the fake IDs Carla has bought them, when Jean-François comes down the hall and grabs Carla by the arm and shakes her, then gets up very close to Giselle's face and spits, "The princess has to go— now!" Carla just laughs, calls her father a "stupid welfare case" and gives him a push out her door, but Giselle has watched this father-daughter interaction play out before and knows it will consume the entire evening, end with Carla's dad remorseful, holding his emaciated red face in his veiny hands, blubbering that he loves his daughter, and with Carla, unforgiving and ashamed of him, going silent; smoking more pot; wordlessly blaming Giselle for seeing the unfiltered version of her life, for the "luck" of Giselle's own asshole father being dead, which has changed everything for her, and for how bad Carla misses her own mother. She might even begrudge Giselle Lazar, whom Carla has said she finds handsome, in a gangster kind of way. Giselle leaves.

Outside, the heavy silence of falling snow makes Giselle feel wide awake. She pulls out her phone to text Gabe, walking in the direction of the street corner where she can grab a cab to his mom's place, but stops herself before the call goes through: she's had three beers; she can't tell how he'll react, smelling it on her. He'll be in the middle of studying, which makes him so anxious. For several minutes Giselle stands on the sidewalk breathing in the cold air, knowing she isn't truly welcome anywhere. She nearly veers right, towards the graveyard where her father is buried. But visiting him there is almost as disappointing as the man himself was. She decides to sneak into her own room through the back door; she can hide out till after breakfast, when Lazar usually leaves for wherever he's got business of the kind no one asks about directly, especially not her mother.

When she steps inside, she hears their music coming from upstairs. Giselle walks quietly through the kitchen. On the island are the remnants of filo pastry snacks, Lazar's leather jacket, his trademark sunglasses, which he wears even in the winter, way up on his forehead, and a suede bag. Quietly, uncertain of her own motive, Giselle walks over and opens the soft bag. There, still and surprising as pearls, she finds a thick stack of bills and a Ziploc of coke.

In the moment it takes to register this sight, Giselle's mind relinquishes control, moving into the back seat. Her body takes over. She takes the cash—all of it. Standing on the cool tile floor with the low hum of her mother's new fridge, the trappings of her mother's confused ambitions closing in around her, Giselle registers only that her hands are full of money. She walks out the back door, closes it very quietly and runs so long and hard she vomits into the toilet of the women's washroom when she gets to the Greyhound station. She buys a ticket, fakes a smile at the harmless-looking driver and takes a seat at the back of the Express that soon leaves, its great wheels crackling across the fresh snow, for Toronto.

She isn't sure what she will do. She expects that she will blow Lazar's money just because she can, because for once something will be hers alone. Then she'll go back, take the heat. Gabe might even be impressed that she would defy Lazar this way. Carla will be amazed; Giselle is casting out—way out, past the men in her life. But by the time the bus has crossed the Port Severn Bridge, she becomes convinced that everything behind her has been frozen solid—the city, her mother, Carla's stuffed animals—and that she has no business returning to such a desolate place. Arriving in downtown Toronto, she checks into the hotel closest to the bus terminal, turns on the TV, takes a chocolate bar and a miniature Heineken from the mini fridge, and lies on the bed. She tries to push away a memory of the last hotel she stayed in, in the Dominican Republic, with her mother and Lazar, but the details of that elaborate suite float to her as she rests, seeing again the waterfall shower and the trays of food delivered each morning—which her mother was careful not to touch. Gabe and his mom had been invited, but of course he had refused to go. He told Giselle he wouldn't leave Sudbury until the day he went to law school, and never on Lazar's dime. But he envied her for going and hated her tan enough for it to trigger one of their fights.

Giselle sleeps deeply and, in the morning, texts Gabe, then her mother and finally Carla, telling each of them that she's sick and will see them later. Then she stomps on her phone until she hears it crack and checks out, paying cash.

It takes two months to learn how to look and act like a local. She buys a series of disposable cells. She acquires fewer clothes than she imagined, but the ones she chooses closely resemble those she has seen on the women who live near the downtown sublet she rents, also in cash. She makes an appointment at an expensive-looking hair salon. She arrives with her long hair teased and streaked blonde and comes out with an angled bob dyed a deep, chestnut brown. At the pharmacy near her place, she follows the advice of a serious-minded beauty consultant and buys wine-coloured lipstick and mocha mascara. She is better-looking than not and, lying about her age and skills, repeating to herself that she is exactly who they will assume she is, gets a temp job as a receptionist for a production company that specializes in science shows. She grows to like the rush of calls during the day. They keep her mind busy.

Occasionally the producers enlist Giselle as an extra for the re-enactments they film for a medical-themed program. In a wig and apron, she becomes a housewife straining her back as she bends to pick up a child's toy. Wearing expensive sneakers, she is filmed running in place. Once, she is just a tongue, another time, an eye. In these moments she relives, as if from the inside, her mother's transformation, from the day her father died until the day she stood dangling the prospect of a new sweater in exchange for Giselle getting out of Lazar's way; at every point, less of her than before.

One of the in-house producers is in his late twenties. He is tall and well-dressed and seems to know a lot about television. He stands at her desk and tells her things about production, about selling shows. He looks nothing like the men Giselle has known well. He is exactly what Carla was talking about. He's what's out there. Occasionally, he asks Giselle questions about herself, to which she provides vague answers. Eventually, he asks her out and she says no. His name is Evan. Seven months into the job, in front of the producer who hired her, Evan tells Giselle that while she is liked at the company, he is concerned that she hasn't shown much initiative in learning to do more than answer phones. People should want more than they have. He offers to take her to an event and introduce her to other TV people—as a favour, he says. Not knowing how to refuse with the big boss looking right at her, Giselle agrees but feels tricked.

Evan takes her to a dinner party at a condominium on the waterfront. Giselle has never been in a place like it. Standing at the front door, she sees gigantic gilded mirrors hanging low on thick wire, zebra skin pillows on a long fat couch, a vase full of crystal balls on a glass coffee table, and velvet curtains that remind her of those in Sudbury's old movie theatre. Behind them are glass doors looking out onto Lake Ontario from thirty floors up.

"Jack," says the host, introducing himself as he extends a hand towards her, smiling. Giselle reaches for it, but only manages to graze his fingers because Jack has caught sight of another woman coming down the hall. "Jennie!" he says much too loudly as Giselle steps aside and into the apartment, giving him room to get to Jennie, whom he grabs with a full-body hug.

"They're a dramatic bunch," says Evan.

During dinner Giselle is silent. She finds the food terrible. Too spicy. And there's no beer. She lets herself imagine how Carla would react. Probably by cupping a hand around her face to hide it, then making a gagging gesture only Giselle would see. Giselle smiles at the idea.

Evan talks about his role at the production company. Everyone seems fascinated. "If this pitch goes ahead, though, I'll be out of there," he says. "Like, enough with the 'one million ways to be healthy' stuff." He puts an invisible gun to his head and pulls the trigger, making a "Poof!" sound. He looks around and gets a lot of nods and chuckles. Then his eyes fall on Giselle, who has been sitting beside him for the length of the meal. It's like he's seeing her for the first time. Giselle is conscious of his face, his worked-out shoulders, and his physical presence, how little it calls to her the way Gabe's did. Evan pauses. "I mean, it's not them, really. Giselle, you're happy there, I know. I just have to find a way to move on. We both should."

"What do you do, Giselle?" says one guest, named Christian, who's wearing little round glasses and a short-sleeved workman's shirt like the ones Carla's father always wore, except clean and pressed.

She tells him she's the receptionist.

Christian looks quickly from left to right and adjusts his fork.

"Yes, yes, she works the phones," says Evan, leaning her way, waving his wineglass at Christian. "So what? Everyone has to start somewhere. She's also on camera. She's been an extra in—what is it, Giselle? Six or seven episodes of *Made of Muscle*? From what I hear from the crew, you make a pretty hot house-wife."

Everyone laughs. Giselle drinks her entire glass of water. As soon as possible, she excuses herself. In the bathroom, looking into the huge track-lit mirror, she feels nauseous. She turns the water on full blast and forces herself to chuck up her spicy supper. She has never done this before; it feels better than she'd expected, which puts her into an awkward, silent alliance with her mother. Later, when Evan drops her off, apologizing for his comment, saying he didn't like that guy Christian's tone, Giselle undoes her seatbelt. The car objects, beeping at her loudly. "What? You're going?" says Evan. "I stood up for you back there."

Bracing herself for resistance, for words or a hand to try to keep her where she is, Giselle gets out quickly, but Evan just drives away. She is left alone, wondering why he didn't push, what keeps people from just taking what they want. The only explanation is that they must not need it badly enough. Giselle heads up the wooden stairs to her apartment, each step sounding hollow. The following Monday, she gives notice at the production company.

She finds a new job while walking through Kensington Market. There's a Help Wanted sign in the window of a busy deli. The manager tells her she can start immediately. The job pays minimum wage but she takes it. Having long since run through her stack of bills, she moves apartments, sharing an attic space in Chinatown with the girl who has the lease. Jill is upbeat, with a serious commitment to the environment and to her boyfriend. She is almost never home. Giselle also cuts her hair and dyes it blonde. She has been sure for some weeks that no one ever filed a missing person report about her. No police, in cars or patrolling on foot, have ever paused to scrutinize her face. Still, she has occasionally been startled seeing someone who looks like her mother, like Lazar, Gabe or Carla. Each time she has wanted to run towards them, and for this reason, she feels she must stay hidden.

Six times a week, in the early morning, she walks to work, going up and across Spadina where noodle and seafood restaurants, hardware supply shops and cheap clothing stores crowd together. During her ten-hour shifts, she is happily busy again: calling out numbers; pulling paper with a snap from big suspended rolls; laying the red, white, brown and jellied meats, the breasts, thighs and ribs, intestines and tongues across the centre; wrapping and tying; then printing out labels and sticking them on. During breaks she puts a few thick slabs of ham between slices of dark rye and runs across the street to stand outside a coffee shop with two other women, all of them in their stained aprons and paper hats. One is an overweight high school dropout. The other is Russian, in her forties. Her name is Gordana and she wears her blonde bangs in a curly bunch. They stick out from under her paper hat like a flower.

"Dat place is a zoo," says Gordana almost every day, and proceeds with a tirade against her husband, who cheats on her, but whom she says she can't leave because he's such a good father.

The high school dropout, Deborah, is nervous and surly at the same time. "They're fuckers," she often says, referring maybe to husbands, maybe to the owners of the deli. Generally, Giselle lets them do the talking. They make her laugh quite a lot, reminding her a little of Carla.

Near the end of shifts, the floor behind the deli counter is dangerous. Everyone ends up sliding around on the day's dropped blood, cheese and ground meat. About five months into the job, overconfident and holding a stack of ribs, Giselle falls hard on her back behind the counter. Everything seizes and she is forced to remain on the floor a long time, the curved ribs scattered where they've fallen like bloody question marks. Everyone gathers, their white hats tilting onto their foreheads, reminding Giselle of an operation scene they staged for *Made of Muscle*. The goo of the floor soaks through her T-shirt.

"Giz-*elle*! Giz-*elle*! You okay?" says Gordana, kneeling,

looking a bit crazed so close up, with her grey eyes and her flower bangs. Stunned with pain, Giselle can't answer.

Eventually her co-workers help her to stand, and Deborah offers to accompany her the five blocks back to her apartment. Slowly, they work their way up the stairs where Giselle lies down on her bed. Deborah repeats her mantra that the owners are fuckers, that they need to clean the floor more often, and that Giselle should try to get some Workers' Comp. Then she goes back downstairs and to the pharmacy to buy some Extra Strength Tylenol. She pours Giselle some water and leaves. Alone in the silence of the dry, overheated attic, the distant sound of traffic on Dundas Street coming in a regular hum, Giselle whimpers a little, downs four of the Tylenols and falls asleep.

Over the next three days she eats next to nothing and lies almost continuously on her bed or on the couch listening to the CBC and dozing, using a steady supply of pills to keep from crying out in pain. Her roommate has gone out of town to attend a large anti-mining demonstration and does not come home. She doesn't need to; her many posters, sticky-tacked to the sloping ceiling of the attic, scream out her every opinion: CLIMATE ACTION NOW! and OUR OCEANS DESERVE BETTER! Giselle has yet to hear Jill talk about mining in Canada, and Giselle has not been tempted to say anything about her father's accident underground.

Giselle's phone rings and her doorbell chimes several times. The women from the deli both text her. "You OK?" and "Call us!!" She writes brief replies but leaves it at that.

Lying completely still, the muscles in her back tight as fists, her jaw twitchy from clenching, Giselle feels helpless against herself. Her body, robbed of its ability to act—to leave, to refuse, to be silent, to turn away—takes a back seat. Her mind, so long glazed, frozen over, begins to pull her, as through a tunnel, back in time—past Gordana's crazed eyes, past Evan's arrogant defense of her, then up the highway to Sudbury, out of the bus station

bathroom where she flushed down the vomit, past even the crucial bag of Lazar's money. The landscape of her life there is petrified, but vivid. Her mind surveys every inch of it, refusing to
stop until she can almost see her mother's leather leggings and
feel, afresh, the certainty of being unwelcome. Time slows. She
feels hollowed out. She finds herself packing some clothes into
a bag, then getting in a taxi, leaving for the Greyhound. Soon
again she is descending into the crater that holds all of Sudbury
like in a nutshell. As the bus pulls into the terminal, it is as cold
and desolate as when she left.

She spends some time in the terminal making phone calls,
then grabs a cab to the city centre. It drops her off at the office of
a Dr. Marc Barth, Orthodontist. A bell tinkles. The receptionist
looks up. Carla, wearing less makeup than a year ago, stares at
Giselle with relief, then resistance. Giselle hasn't eaten since yesterday morning. Her back is on fire. "Can I lie down?"

Carla brings her to a quiet room, where Giselle presumes the
dentist must perform his operations, and sneaks her some Tylenol 3s. Giselle sleeps a long time. When she wakes up, daylight
is already fading. Through a window she sees a blue-hued snow
bank. Carla comes in holding both their coats. "I'll drive."

Easing herself into Carla's car, Giselle feels a bit high from
the pain pills, but also cold and alert. "Your mother's still crazy
worried, you know—" Carla starts, but trails off.

"I called."

Carla shakes her head. "Yeah, well. Good for you. You
could've died. I told her, I said, 'Don't worry. She and I haven't
gone a week—a day—without talking since we're six. She'll find
a way to let me know when she's coming home.' But you didn't.
I mean, you erased your Facebook account. Who does that? The
only funny part was hearing how they laid into Gabe."

Giselle squints involuntarily.

"Yeah. See? He still exists. Laz and your Mom, they hounded
him. They figured he's the one who made you go. Of course he
pretended to be cool about it. Asshole. He's with some chick

from school now. Tried to blow me off when I saw him, but I went right up, got in his face, said, 'You didn't even try to find her, you piece of shit!'"

Giselle rubs her forehead with her hand. "Neither did you."

"Right. Because you wanted to be found. By me. Fuck you. You know how many times I saw a car parked outside my building this year? Lazar's boys, making sure you weren't coming around. I said nothing. I did nothing. And your mom still doesn't know, in case you're wondering. About Gabe. They'd murder him, I swear. Beat him to death with one of his fucking textbooks."

Giselle can't help but smile. "Can we go to the slag heap?"

Carla hesitates. "What, now?"

"I just want to sit there."

"After all this time. Why?"

"Please."

Carla tsks loudly but does a U-turn, and they drive to the place where, as girls, they would take their bikes to watch as the hot slag—waste left over from the city's mines—poured down the hills of black debris. They pull up just as a great cauldron rolls down the track and stops. Abruptly, it spins forward on its steel pivots and vomits out its filthy contents, now glowing brilliant liquid gold.

Giselle and Carla sit in silence as the slag begins its long leak downwards, spreading out across a section of the hill in rivulets, forming a shape like extended, glowing tree roots, or like the map of a nervous system on fire, but cooling at the ends, already beginning its slow return to a solid state of waste. Looking straight ahead, they let the car's heater warm the air between them. Then Carla, one high-heeled leather boot propped up on the door-side runner, lights a joint and opens her window a crack, exhaling in that general direction. "It's still friggin' rad."

"It is," says Giselle, dropping her head and feeling, finally, Carla's presence, as though her friend has just now allowed it to be shared. Giselle becomes aware that she is breathing more easily than she has since the accident. The muscles in her back are loosening. She reaches over and Carla lets the joint go into her pinched fingers. Giselle takes a deep drag and waits for another cauldron of slag to come shining over the top of the heap.

CATCH

Cats aren't like other animals. Cat owners know this. They know cats can slot through an opening or wring themselves out like there's no bones inside. They know cats are extremely horny and that they have an extra sense, some kind of cross between whiskers and smell. But I didn't have a clue about them until I took the job at the animal hospital. There, I learned that the wilder the cat, the more these descriptions apply, which makes ferals a superspecies. There's nothing extra on them. They are barely there, physically. But sense-wise, they are honed, and that makes them dangerous and near-psychic. "Always a step ahead," as Gerald put it. "Like Eichmann in Argentina."

I had my doubts. I've always hated psychics. Jess called them sometimes using those 1-900 numbers. I knew no TV psychic could tell her anything that she didn't want them to, or that she hadn't indirectly let them know. But Jess was hungry for prediction. Even when she didn't have a pot to piss in, she'd still phone up when the number came on TV. All that money. I told her, "Jess, here's the future, free of charge: you're going to live, get old, get even older, and die." The last time I said this, Jess looked up from the TV and narrowed her eyes at me. "More than you can say for your cats." I thought that was uncalled-for, considering that "my cats" were paying Jess's half of the rent and installments on the TV. But she wasn't wrong.

Gerald is the one who taught me about catching cats. He'd been catching for the hospital longer than anyone else, so he was assigned to be my mentor. I can still see him our first night, pulling over in front of our building an hour late, squealing to a stop in a truck painted blood orange with blue steaks along the bottom that flamed out yellow at the rear. Spoilers, molded cab, oversized floodlights. He made an entrance. Gerald wasn't much older than me, maybe twenty-eight, but he was retro, with shiny hair going straight back from his forehead in a wave, and a short-sleeved shirt with a dragon snaking over one shoulder. Between the outfit and the truck, Gerald seemed to know how he wanted the world to perceive him, and that made me feel childish because I didn't. I was wearing exactly what the boss, Dr. Van Hurst, had told me to: jeans, a long-sleeved shirt and my old leather jacket. I got in the truck with the long Kevlar gloves I'd been required to buy and closed the door. Gerald looked me up and down and smiled. "Newbie."

"That's why I'm here, right? To learn."

"Oh man, you bet you're going to learn." He reached over and I pulled away, fully expecting one of those slaps on the shoulder that men use to diminish you. But Gerald kept reaching and gave me an unexpectedly friendly double tap on the upper arm. Then he picked up an iPod that was connected to his stereo. "Doctor Frankenstein down at The Pet Ritz, he tell you what this is really about?" he said, running his thumb around the circular touch pad to choose some rockabilly song that was too jumpy for my tastes.

"He gave me the basics," I said over springy steel guitar.

Gerald nodded. "Basics." He didn't like the word, or maybe Van Hurst rubbed him the wrong way. He steered the truck into a noisy U-turn and revved up, bringing us towards the main artery that connected my east-end neighbourhood with the downtown core. "Did he tell you cats are mean?" he said, driving fast. There was a dried baby alligator hanging from Gerald's rearview mirror, and it swung rapidly, strongly emphasizing the point about meanness. "Mean as anything? Mean as people? My policy is no mercy."

We were quiet after that, listening to the music. I watched the slivers of orange streetlight slide over the dashboard and our laps and considered what I had gotten myself into.

We exited onto a major road that parallels the lakeshore and Gerald started to talk again. "Ferals. Permanent escapees. Kidney hoarders. Pick your own term of endearment. I don't care. But they have the city mapped out with scent like a war zone."

He slowed down as we rode past a bunch of warehouses. Some of these had obviously been renovated and had stylish signs on them for tech companies, design firms. But as we kept moving, more and more of the warehouses were decrepit. We pulled off the road and idled a while in a cracked paved lot. Away from the streetlights, the night altered weeds growing along the warehouse walls so they looked like long grey feathers.

"I'm not religious," said Gerald, killing the motor and reaching behind the seat for his gloves. "Not interested in souls. I work three jobs to keep this truck on the road. That's my thing." He stopped for a second and looked at me carefully. "Van Hurst can give you any bullshit line he wants. I'm not against the people who spoil pets. When I get rich, I'll probably go around paying people to cut the nuts off humans if that's what my furry friend wants. But you have to stay unsentimental, alright? It's a paycheque."

I was holding my gloves tightly on my lap. "I get it," I said.

I've only had one pet in my life. A goldfish I won at the fair that came to our town every summer. I won it in the game where you throw a ping-pong ball, and if it lands in a fishbowl you get to keep the fish. I remember that year I knew my father wouldn't have any money to send me to the midway, so I swiped two fives from my aunt's till, and me and my friend Derek went down and rode the Salt 'n Pepper Shaker, then calculated which games we should play for maximum duration and chances at a prize. Derek threw baseballs at a cutout wall. I blew my wad on the shooting range, then had just enough left for the fish game. I actually won two and gave one to Derek, but his died within hours. Not mine. I changed his water as soon as I got home and called him Eddie, after Eddie Van Halen. I'd watch him swim and I thought about how he was supposed to have been born in an ocean, how he hadn't been given the chance.

Eddie seemed to thrive. He would eye me through bent glass as he rounded his bowl. That eye was sharp. Then one day I woke up and he was dead. So I flushed him. I don't remember feeling anything much. If I think back now, I can't say I loved that fish. How can a fish take love? Gerald was right about that much: animals don't have souls. I remember my father, when I came downstairs, how he commented that I looked sick. I told him about Eddie and he laughed until it turned into coughing. "They're not exactly built to last." Then he kept on walking into the living room. He had on these really old pyjamas that were practically see-through in the ass. I hated the thought of seeing my father's ass. I knew he hadn't intended to be mean. Most of what he said was directed at himself. But I felt like I had to get out of there, get away from the couch where he always sat, which smelled like old newspapers. The toilet was still running from when I'd flushed it. I visualized myself smashing it with a sledgehammer, but instead I went back to my room and closed the door.

The back of Gerald's truck was devoted to the job of catching cats and had everything we needed. We couldn't use chemicals because it would mess up the animals, he said. The hospital didn't want to waste time cutting into a cat with pickled kidneys. You had to use nets, two kinds of traps and a cat grasper, which was a long pole with a trigger controlling pincers on the end. Gerald said if I got as good as he was, I wouldn't have to worry much about getting scratched up or bit, and I'd never have to cash in on the just-in-case rabies shots they were giving me at the hospital. He kept telling me to relax and to "think like a cat."

"Cats don't get attached, alright? They live with you for years, free room and board, tickles on the belly, whatever. Then, one day: gone. They're not attachable. Ferals especially. They're already aware of us, you know that? Oh yeah. They know. These things are living at ground level. And they're about as eager to get into one of our cages as we'd be to get hauled off to Rikers for twenty hard—or to be hauled off to a church to be married." He winked.

We'd only just met and Gerald didn't even know about Jess. It really freaked me out, like all that psychic cat business had rubbed off on him.

Jess suggested we get married less than a month after we moved in together, which was about a month and two days after we'd met at a noisy, ugly club my friend Derek forced me to go to. Everything was in fast-forward from the start and I didn't know what to make of her being in such a rush.

"You're kidding," I said, when she raised the subject, then tried to recover. "It's that we just got into this. Let me get some work and some money together and we'll see."

That was enough to massage the moment, but even after I got my first job, at a pet store, I didn't bring up marriage like I said I would. It got to be like a black eye no one wants to mention because it came from a sucker punch and it's embarrassing.

Then one night, I was lying beside Jess on the futon feeling good and relaxed. She had the sheets covering her up to the waist, and I liked seeing her naked chest stretched out with the pink nipples pointed towards her armpits. Jess was pretty in a way I'd never been close to before. She had a triangle chin and small shoulders, like a bird. She was nervous and fierce, with eyes that didn't give away much about the person inside. She reached across me for an unlit joint I'd left on her laptop on the floor and sparked up. "Where do the guinea pigs in your store come from?" she asked me.

"I've told you. The store has its suppliers."

"They never get outside?"

"If someone buys them, they go wherever people want them to go."

Jess smoked, considering this. "We've only ever had dogs. Yorkshire terriers. My mom's been obsessed with them forever. When I had friends over, they'd ooh and ahh, but the dogs were never mine. More like a buffer between my mom and everybody else." Jess got quiet, exhaling. Then she passed me the joint like she'd suddenly remembered that I was still there. "I think animals should have their own space. They shouldn't be an excuse or a distraction for people."

"Agreed."

"Maybe you could get us a pair of guinea pigs."

I didn't know how to respond. I regretted ever telling Jess about the pet mills the store used and how little the animals there had seen the sun.

Jess kept pecking at the joint, bringing it to her lips over and over. I knew her mother was distant and her father went along with it, and that these things caused Jess pain. But she didn't really know about bad families. Her parents were still together and they called her all the time. Yet she was the one who seemed to need to turn us into a family, while me, with the non-existent parents and no one else exactly beating down my door to ask what's up, I could see the value in keeping some distance. At the same time, part of me knew I should jump at the chance to be with someone like Jess, someone who believed so much in the future. I said, "Let's get married." And we did. Derek was my witness, and Jess's best friend Sam was hers. We bought a cake at Dairy Queen, then Jess and I stayed up all night looking at each other. We couldn't believe it.

I was weirded out, then, that first night, when Gerald piped up about marriage. I didn't bother to say whether I was or wasn't, and by the time the words had left his mouth, I could tell Gerald had lost interest.

He explained how to set a drop trap, which we did,

camouflaging it with some scrub bush. The cats would walk in and take the bait, he said, then all we had to do was come and get them, transfer them to the cage, and bango!—into the back of the truck. But cats are wise to traps, he said, and you also need to get out there and hunt with your net. Gerald handed me one, along with the cat grasper.

We snuck around the area for about an hour and a half before we spotted anything. It was early fall and unusually warm. Everything seemed strange in the night, and I felt like I was somewhere I'd never been before, a different country almost, on a mission. I had a lot of questions, but Gerald gave off a vibe like, "shut the fuck up," so I followed him as he stepped across the open lot, then along one of the warehouse walls, further and further though the dark.

Suddenly, he stopped in front of me. I looked hard into the distance and saw: a cat, chewing on something outside an open dumpster. It was scrawny, its shoulder blades sticking up in defined triangles. Gerald signaled for me to stay put, then started walking forward towards the dumpster with the net. The cat was pretty immersed in what it was doing, and Gerald was light on his feet, creeping along in his crazy shirt. I figured the cat wasn't aware of him at all, but when Gerald got close enough, it started to crouch down and hissed. "Easy," Gerald said, then reached into his pocket and pulled something out. He lobbed it towards the cat, which made the animal jump. But it didn't run and actually got closer, pushing at the food with its paw. The distraction was all Gerald needed. In a second he had the weighted net up and out in a wide arc as he ran and threw it over the cat. Then he stepped down on as much of the edges as he could while yelling at me to bring him the grasper. When I ran in close enough, he reached back like a relay runner for a baton; I passed him the handle and he put those pincers over the net and around the cat's neck.

"You're a pretty puss," Gerald said, and pushed down hard on the pole that plugged in like an upside-down divining stick over the cat's neck. The cat yowled in pain. Its ribs rolled under the fur like a wave, the eyes flashed, and it was winding and unwinding its narrow torso like a snake, thrashing under the net. It seemed angry with itself for taking the bait, for not running when it had the chance.

"He put his stomach first," said Gerald, as if reading my mind, keeping the animal in place. "Hold this while I get the truck."

I took the grasper.

"Hold'm just like that, and for Christ's sake, don't let up."

Gerald backed away and I was alone with the cat. From above, its head had a geometric shape, like a hexagon where the two front points were the brow bones. I could feel his anger come up the stick and through my gloves. I imagined its kidneys pulsing inside its body. For a second, I had a real strong urge to raise and open the pincers and let it go. I didn't feel sorry for it. Just something about its wildness under my power made the idea of freedom come into my head. I thought of my long-lost goldfish Eddie.

Gerald pulled up quick enough. His slid a cage out of a plywood box that was built into the back and got me to coax the cat inside with the grasper. When the door was secure, he put his boot on the cage. The cat tried to reach up and claw him, but couldn't get a paw through the tight grid. "Man over beast, bro," said Gerald, and gave the cage a sharp downward kick. The cat crouched and stayed there.

We drove back to where we'd first parked and got out, waiting out of sight for two more hours. Twice we saw cats run across our path, but they were gone too soon to do anything. "They know," said Gerald, nodding meaningfully at me.

"What do they know?"

"The hospital. They smell it on us." He smiled, and when he did, he was good-looking. It crossed my mind that I wouldn't invite him over to meet Jess anytime soon.

He'd just started talking about the sound system in his truck when Gerald's ears perked up at a snapping sound: something was in the trap. It turned out to be a bigger cat, a stray, fatter than the first one. He was banging around like crazy, and the way he behaved created an impression of fear more than anger. Gerald chuckled and showed me how to get the cage door matched up to the trap's door without putting myself within scratching distance, and also how to slide back the divider, which is a metal comb that you use to push the cat closer and closer to the entrance of the cage. When the cat was in there, I snapped shut the door, covered the cage with a towel, and we put it into the back of the truck with the first one.

"Know what?" said Gerald. He was all flushed as he got into the driver's seat and reached back behind him to put away his gloves. "That's enough for tonight." He pulled out a big bottle of something and sprayed it around the cab, which made me sneeze. "Let's get drunk," he said, and put the truck into reverse.

I stayed on with Gerald two weeks. I learned that dumpsters are better places to find cats than almost any, that it's difficult—but possible—to carry catnip or canned mackerel in your pockets without smelling like it yourself, that feral cats have favourite places to mark their territory, like tree stumps, corners of open lots, doorways. If you're patient enough, you can see them there. Gerald showed me how to manage the nets and grasper on my own, and how to look for cat nests without scaring away all the occupants. The real key to good catching, Gerald said, was to keep shaking up your routine. Don't let a single colony of cats figure out your methods. If you catch a female, be extra careful. And if you value your vehicle like he did, he said, bring a lot of anti-scent spray.

I also started dropping the cats off at the hospital. The waiting room for the emergency department was always air-conditioned to near-freezing, even though the weather was finally turning and it was a waste. The room was packed with depressed-looking owners staring through the holes of beige plastic carriers at their limp pets. Birds. Dogs. Iguanas. And cats. Lots of cats.

Everything about the hospital was expensive-looking. Even the small, pink-rimmed halogen lights that lined the hall I followed deeper into the hospital. It always gave me a weird feeling to go through that hall past the big blow-up photos they had of dogs running through fields, and pampered cats with big, wet eyes looking right at me.

Sometimes, I would bump into Dr. Van Hurst on his way in for a day's work, his white lab coat neatly folded over his arm. He looked like he played a doctor on TV. "Getting what we need, Roger?" he'd say. Once, he stopped me to show off a picture of a little girl grinning, resting a hand on her cat in what looked like a recovery room. "This child is going to have her pet around for a long time, thanks to the work you're doing, Rog." I managed to smile and give him a "Yes, sir."

I didn't like to think too much about what happened to the cats I brought in after the door to the holding room closed behind me. I'm not stupid. I knew some nurse would pull the towel off the cage. I knew that within a day a kidney would be out and sewn into someone's pet. I didn't want to know what that operation looked like, and tried to stay focused instead on what it was worth to the families, and now me.

Following Gerald's advice, I started going out in my own car on shift. I also started thinking like a cat. I wasn't sleeping well during the day, so I stayed up, wired on caffeine, then toked up to calm down in the evenings before my shift. I started eating more meat—which didn't make much sense, but I thought it suited my new lifestyle. I noticed how I was more and more happy when Jess had already left for school by the time I came home, and I could just lie down in the dark and think. But I also couldn't wait to get her pants off when she got back. In my dreams I saw a lot of animals—not just cats, but dogs and birds.

A couple times a week, Gerald and I would meet up for drinks. It got to be a ritual, with Gerald doing most of the talking. "When it comes down to it Rog, why do we bother with anything more than the basics, you know?" he'd say. Or he'd want me to help him picture himself on various adventures. "I've been thinking about the idea of living on an island somewhere. Somewhere I could still have my truck, though. What do you think?" Mostly, Gerald didn't expect me to answer these questions. I didn't mind. Gerald was interesting and he got me thinking a lot about animals and what the differences are between them and us. I remember sitting on the john one evening after a few beer and just looking at my own hands, contemplating all the wild things a human is capable of. I pretended to paw the air. When I flexed my fingers like into claws, my hands looked as if they belonged to someone else. Later, I was frying up a steak in the kitchen and caught Jess looking at me from the living room like she'd picked up on a change in my energy. When she saw me looking back, she turned away and cranked up the volume on the TV.

Things with Gerald changed suddenly. This was a few months into the job. I had just dropped off three cats at the hospital one early morning and was headed home when I noticed his truck following me. He stayed behind me all the way to my place, then got out and walked up to my car door.

"What's going on, Gerald?" I said, rolling down my window.

He showed me deep scratches on his shoulder. "Female," he said. "All claws. I didn't bring her in."

"What do you mean?"

"What do you think I mean?" he said, putting his big hands on the bottom of the window and leaning over. "It was me against her." Gerald might have been drinking. One thick strand of his hair had fallen out of its wave and was dangling over his eye.

He stayed propped up like that, blocking out the morning sun, as if he wanted me to respond. But I was too busy imagining the ways Gerald might have dealt with a terrified cat in the middle of the night with no one else around to see. I got the feeling, again, like Gerald might be reading my mind, and I felt, suddenly, that I was in the presence of a dangerous person. I glanced over at the front door of our low-rise. Jess came to the small front window of the apartment, which was on the second floor, and peeked out. Gerald must have sensed something, because he turned and gave her a long look until she stepped away into the shadows.

"What do you think you've got going for you, Roger?"

"What do you mean?"

"Life. Besides this job. I mean life. What do you have?"

This didn't sit well with how tired I was feeling, or the fact that Gerald had followed me all the way to my place to ask me such an asshole question, or the way things had been going with Jess, which he knew nothing about.

"My life's fine."

"You know what I see, Roger? I look at you and I see someone who's happy enough to be led into a cage and have the blanket pulled down."

"Fuck you," I said, but I don't think I sounded very convincing because Gerald laughed. He stood up straight and tapped the roof of my car in his friendly way, which I could now see was an aspect of him that existed alongside the rest unintegrated, like the way lion trainers can get right up close to an adult male for a hug and to have their faces licked, but later will stand outside the cage and chuck a hunk of raw meat inside and watch as the animal tears it up, covering itself in blood. "You know what I really want?" Gerald said. "A cabin. Have you read *Into the Wild*? I should bring a copy to you, man. It's unreal." Like everything was fine again. Maybe Gerald was schizophrenic.

Through my rearview mirror, I watched him walk back to his truck. As he went, I made out some dark red splatters on the back of his pants below the knees. Blood. He drove up beside me. "See you next shift, Rog," he said, and threw something jingly through my window.

I nodded just so he'd go away, then looked down to see that I had a little white collar with tags on my lap.

Jess didn't like my new out-all-night, meat-eating, cat freak persona. She was also preoccupied with her own issues, which made her even more like a bird. If I touched her wrong during sex, she wanted me out and off her right away. She ate almost nothing. She perched in front of the TV all day and blew off the college classes her parents had paid for. She was basically miserable.

"What's going on," I said, one day, just before leaving for a shift.

"I think I need to go and stay at Sam's a while."

"Why would you do that? We're married."

"What do you care, anyway? You're sucking the life out of this place."

I left for work without another word, and when I got home in the morning, Jess was gone. She left me a note that said she was sorry, she didn't know what was going on, but she wasn't sure we should've got married, and she didn't know if she loved me or if she'd really been trying to get attention from her parents, and she was scared because she'd racked up a bunch of money on her mom's credit card, and she needed to be someplace normal so please don't call Sam's, okay?

Two nights later, I found myself inside a warehouse where someone had bent back one of the corrugated bay doors. I had a good feeling, so I set my traps inside, wandering in with my net, my grasper hanging from my belt and some catnip in my pocket. It was ages before I saw anything. Finally, a green eye lit up like an LED across my flashlight's field, then out again. I followed the motion with my light and saw the cat patting soundlessly towards a corner. I was getting pretty good with the net by then. I threw some nip and moved in its direction. I saw him get his back up and I could feel the hostility in his pose. I killed the light a second, thinking I would let him settle in with the food, let him put his stomach first. I stepped closer, slowly. My eyes adjusted in time to see him bolt away with some of the nip. He ran right past me and up some stairs. I followed, rushing past my empty trap.

The cat didn't have many options. The stairs led to a small loft from which there was no other way down that I could see. I went up and backed him into a corner, threw down some more food, then hesitated. His eyes and his body were feral-looking. But he was shaking with fear, like a domesticated. I jumped forward and threw out the wide net. The cat didn't know which way was out. I came forward with my grasper as fast as I could, but before I could secure it, the thing jumped right off the ground under the net and swiped me above the knee. I recoiled, shocked by pain, but I knew I had to stay there to hold down the edge, so I reached out with the grasper and managed to get the neck secured.

"Fucker!" I screamed, pushing down harder on the pincers and watching the cat being subdued into a crouch. Its claws were still out and it wanted to do me more damage. I felt my anger spill out into that handle and down the cat's spine. For a second I thought I would just crack its neck, and I realized it would probably feel good and natural.

Then I heard. Faint meowing. I kept pressure on the grasper but turned and looked into the darkest corner of the loft. I coaxed the cat into the nearby trap, and, as I did, I realized it was a female, with big full teats. I pushed down the trap's door and secured it, then pulled up my pant leg to examine the scratches on my left thigh. Bright red blood was running in four evenly spaced trickles towards my sock.

I pointed the flashlight and walked forward with the grasper. When I got close, I could see some debris and a lump of something furry. Kittens. A nestful. I bent down, wincing at the pain in my legs. They were all dead. The fur fallen off in places. Sharp teeth sticking out and some with their grey eyes still wide open. In a moment, I saw so many things bundled together: the blow-ups at the hospital of the Hallmark pets, Van Hurst reaching into a split-open stray with a scalpel for his $3,000 kidney, Gerald leaning into my car window with blood under his nails, one mouth in a matted head, attached to an abscessed shoulder, opening, and my own hands, reaching. Behind me, the mother cat rattled the trap.

I hurried through the automatic emergency-room doors. It was already morning and people were walking in, chitchatting, holding coffee cups or file folders or sick pets in carriers. Two steps into the building, I saw the boss.

"Dr. Van Hurst!"

He looked at me, saw the stains on my pants and the towel covering my hands, grabbed my arm hard and pulled me out of the waiting room and into an elevator. A young girl walking by with a pet turtle gave me a long, confused look before the doors closed, making her disappear.

"Don't cause scenes, Roger," said Van Hurst, letting go of my arm.

"I've got a kitten. It needs help. It's not a donor. It's—"

"Alright. Take it to Janice in admissions. I'm sure they can look at it later."

"It's dying, Dr. Van Hurst."

The elevator stopped on the fourth floor and the doors opened. Van Hurst took my arm again with a strong hand that left me no option, pulling me out and down the hall to his office. Inside, he closed the door behind us. "Let me see," he said.

On his desk, I laid down the kitten and pulled off the towel.

"Jesus. Why did you bring this here?" he said.

"I wanted to save it," I said, and realized, even as the words came out of my mouth, that the kitten was already dead, lying between us on Van Hurst's big wood desk in the morning light that suddenly seemed all wrong. Just beside its body was a professional picture of Van Hurst with his wife and kids at some barn with two golden retrievers.

I picked up the towel and placed it, properly, over the kitten, then looked up at Van Hurst, who had stepped behind his desk and was talking into his phone. I had a vision of myself lunging over the desk and strangling him. But I shook it off, turned and walked out.

In the parking lot, the air was still biting and the sun hurt my eyes. I called Sam's.

"Yeah?" Jess said, when she got on the line. Her voice was sleepy.

"I'm done work," I said. Just then, Gerald's truck pulled up closer to Emergency. He went around the back to pull two cages from his plywood box, but not before he lifted a comb to fix his hair in his rearview mirror. I turned away.

"So?" Jess said.

"Jess?"

"What?"

"I don't know, I was thinking about daytime. How I'd like to get back to spending more time in the day."

"I'm in bed. Can this wait?"

"I think we should get some plants. For the place. Can I come get you and we'll go shopping?"

"I'm fried, Roger. I talked to my mother last night. Sam and me got stoned after that…. I have school. Can you call me tomorrow?"

"Oh, sure," I said, and hung up. It was strange. I regretted leaving the kitten where I had, but I also didn't want to go back to the hospital for anything. So I walked to my car and tried to figure out what kind of plants I should get, how many it would take to make our apartment greener.

FIDDLE

With some difficulty they locate the fiddle player's house and, receiving no answer at the front door, wander around the back to find the famous young man sitting on the steps of a wide deck wearing work boots, dirty shorts and nothing more. Facing away, he holds both arms straight out from his sides, ten long fingers moving rapidly as if over invisible, suspended keyboards. Seawater makes a great, regular roar as it surges far below the cliff that puts an abrupt end to his property. Maybe this is why he does not seem to hear Beth say hello the first or second time she calls his name. She wonders if he's high and, if he is, what he thinks he's doing with those arms (not even fiddling moves), whether he will be alarmed by the sight of her and of Anthony, whose camera dangles heavily, perhaps threateningly, from a shoulder strap. She knows that her and Anthony's presence tends to inspire suspicion in people. It's a healthy fear, she thinks, of having one's guts placed on display, but one she knows from experience is nearly always overcome by people's easily stirred belief that they belong on TV. This isn't cynicism. Only a reminder to wait and see.

"HELLO!" she yells again, upon which the fiddle player finally turns, letting his hands fall onto completely hairless, tanned legs. In contrast, a patch of hair, quite red, decorates his chest like stretched yarn. He offers his guests a stiff salute. Beth returns a wave, flashing forward through the day as it's about to unfold until she is back at the hotel in Gander, her shoot tapes full of this scenery and Colin's underwhelming story of talent, success, addiction and withdrawal from the world, a story easily gleaned by anyone with an internet connection, but which Beth and Anthony have come thousands of miles to get from the source because that's something totally different. Good TV.

She steps forward. Colin lets a quirky, maybe nervous ripple run over the left side of his full lips. It doesn't amount to a smile. The record company representative who pitched the sit-down said Colin was "dying" to talk. From this, Beth's boss surmised that he's scheming a comeback, that the interview was a must-do.

But now, meeting her halfway across the damp green lawn, Colin shakes Beth's hand only briefly, half-heartedly, then Anthony's, as if they've come to read his meter.

"Well. You made it," he says, too loudly to be justified even by the nearly digital sound effects of the waves below. He is smaller than Beth thought he'd be. Finer boned and with whiter teeth. A thick black plug stretches each earlobe. "What'd it take you? I told 'em to tell you two solid hours."

"It was all good," says Anthony, though they got lost twice, the GPS having become useless when they wandered off into "unverified territory." Beth just smiles. It's not Anthony's habit to admit to mistakes.

Their reclusive host doesn't seem pleased. "Try that road after November 1st," he says, his eyes briefly darting towards Anthony.

"Oh, I bet!" says Anthony, oblivious to the dare, shaking his head and smiling as if picturing himself tackling a blizzard to ride that winding highway in winter. Anthony is big, long-limbed. He always shows up early, always wears expensive black camera-person's clothes, sunglasses and his polished wedding ring. Loves driving. Loves following complicated directions to get where they have to go. Anthony is the most practical person Beth knows. A pro. But in their three years as colleagues, she has never once heard him express an interest in their subject matter: music. She often wonders about this, and about Anthony's willingness to take orders from her. She's just over half his age and has exactly one more year of formal education.

"To the house then?" says Colin, jabbing a thumb towards his large, wood-shingled home. The thumb is nicotine-stained (the teeth shouldn't be so white, Beth can't help thinking), the whole hand sinewy, a hand that can draw a bow across fiddle strings like few others, that used to make Colin lots of money. Beth has never much enjoyed Celtic music, and Colin's albums, which she listened to while preparing for this assignment, sound to her like awkward mash-ups of that genre with unchecked rock licks. Beth, who plays piano seriously enough to have once wished she could do it professionally, prefers melody.

Colin takes them back to the front entrance the long way, walking them around the far side of the house past a row of thorny wild rose bushes. He's suddenly very chatty, talking and gesturing non-stop all the way, like a recording, describing one aspect of the house after another, occasionally yanking up the shorts that threaten to expose the crack of his thin ass. In a gravelly, jumpy voice and slight Maritime sing-song accent, he tells them how he helped design the place, how these antique windows were shipped from St. John's, how he only used wood and craftspeople from Newfoundland. Beth can feel Anthony's interest in these practicalities perking alongside his total disinterest in the speaker. He responds with cool nods.

They enter and walk single file through the huge, bare foyer where a polished wooden staircase rises to the left, then proceed down a hall that gives onto several rooms. Beth spots none of the gold records or hand-shaking shots with the Queen that she's rolled her eyes at in other, similar vanity houses. No record collection at all, actually. The only hint they get of the fiddler's past is a photograph, apparently reprinted from the internet and taped to a half-open door. It's of an old fiddle player, a wiry man who seems half asleep as he leans on a wooden stump playing for a handful of people: a mother and baby, an unsmiling grandmother in a peaked headscarf, and two men with matching hand-rolled cigarettes dangling from their bottom lips, one of them caught lethargically pressing his palms into a clap. Anthony, who's into history and anything old, zeroes in on it. "Is this your father?" he asks.

Beth sees Colin physically shutter before explaining in a reverential tone that this is Émile Benoît, the province's late fiddle legend. He stares at the picture a moment too long, as if lost in its story. Although Colin doesn't seem high, there is something off about his face. He doesn't blink much. Everything is tensed. Beth's heard stories. About huffy exits from interviews. Upended hotel rooms. Blatant sexual behaviour on stage. She's read that people were surprised when he moved back to Newfoundland because they hate him here for being queer, loud and wasted. She considers the dream she had last night, in which Colin offered her cocaine from a foot-high mound, after which he thrust his entire face into it, coming up powdered and ghastly. If only. That would be a coup. This guy is not cocaine crazy, not anymore. Washed-up Hicksville crazy, maybe. A difficult interview, very probably. She'll be a pro about it, Anthony-style.

Except that Anthony is off today. He wouldn't let her listen to one of Colin's early recordings out loud on the drive, asking her to use her earbuds, saying the noise would distract him. Now he keeps missing Colin's cues. His forefinger remains pressed thoughtlessly on the edge of the Benoit picture, obviously one of Colin's prized possessions. "The guy must've been really old here," he says.

Colin just ignores the remark. He turns his back, moving into the light-flooded kitchen. Beth realizes that she is in the middle of nowhere with the world's two most incompatible people. She tries to catch Anthony's eye to judge whether he's been offended by Colin's rebuff, but he refuses to look back. She's recently started to understand that for Anthony, whose gaze is his livelihood, not looking can be the ultimate fuck-you. And this has made her wonder how many times she's been told off by him without knowing so.

Entering the kitchen, Colin goes over to his sink and runs water through the built-in filter. "So. Where do we do this?" he asks, handing Beth and Anthony each a full glass.

Beth, who can feel her pits sweating—contrary to what she's been told to expect, the Newfoundland August morning is already hot—eagerly gulps the tasteless water down. "I read that you have a recording studio here."

Colin drums his counter with both hands in a startling crescendo. "How 'bout we go back outside? I've got a dock."

"Outside. Okay. Sure. That's a possibility," she says, though she's been hoping for a more controlled environment.

She wants to frame the shot with some of Colin's renowned, passed-down-for-generations fiddles. "But if we do go in that direction, outdoors I mean, it would be great if you could bring out one of your instruments."

"I don't play them, so what's the point?" Colin scratches energetically at the stubble shadowing the left side of his jaw. "They were supposed to talk to you about that, see. They didn't give me more than a day's notice, or I could've contacted you about it, but obviously that's not how they work with me now."

"Oh," says Beth, stupidly, doing the math. It's been over two weeks since the record company emailed her with their pitch. Beth assumed the show could take or leave Colin McDermott. Who cares about fiddle music? But her boss, Judith, said Yes yes, you must must go, sweeps is coming up. Judith created the show Beth works for in the 1980s, back when the idea of music journalism on TV seemed like a lasting undertaking. The show has been shriveling like a salted leech in recent years; no one under twenty-five watches TV for music anymore. An ex-punk, Judith has taken its unraveling like a man; she is now a seething pit of anger overlaid with a ravenous obsession with "the get." She'll book any celebrity—even Canadian, non-celebrity celebrities. And she yells. Beth came along well after Judith was considered someone good to work for. Judith hired her because she still esteems musical ability above all, and technically Beth has that. Ironically, lucking into the job forced Beth to put her music on hold. At first she missed it. TV producing felt like a bizarre ritual of being brought face to face with the people Beth most wished she could be: successful musicians. She nearly quit. Then work became a habit. It was money, travel. Successful musicians love talking about music, too. Beth charmed them. Then she started to hate the limited intimacy she could achieve this way. The discrepancy in status was sickeningly vast. Eventually she stopped mentioning her own musical background altogether.

Rumour now is the network will cancel the show after the current season. Beth fears this. She hasn't got even the basics of a music career to return to. She needs her job. If someone as successful as Colin, who's sold enough albums to retire at age twenty-eight, can't even give her a glimpse of his instruments, then he shouldn't have let them come at all, regardless of who set up the shoot.

"Yes. They did tell me you're not playing anymore," she says, trying to sound like nothing can surprise her. "I've read so much about your fiddles, though. They convey a stronger sense of history than anything else we can put in the piece—even this property. They could just be beside you. For the shot."

Colin's unblinking eyes pan left and right, but after a long pause and a hard tug on a section of his thick hair, he nods, says he'll need a few minutes, and excuses himself to go to his studio, which is in the garage. Beth relaxes. She and Anthony go back up the drive to the van to haul out the rest of their gear.

"I can't figure him out," says Beth, reaching in for the shoot tapes, which she's carefully labelled. Counting them, she recognizes in herself an old resentment. Of Colin's wealth, the draw that brings dollars in return for performance and then, eventually, people like her as witnesses, people he can say "yes" or "no" to as he pleases. She thinks of the contrast with her life. Her own decisions are being made without any witnesses. This privacy now strikes her as extremely confining. "Did you see that old couch in his kitchen?" she asks, trying to shake away the suffocating feeling. "I bet he sleeps on that thing. God. What's he doing here? What are we doing here if he's never going to play again?"

She doesn't expect Anthony to answer; instead he performs one of his patented shoulder shrugs. Colin could be the blasé European pop star they shot last week on a press junket, or the achingly honest singer-songwriter whose cancer treatment Judith arranged for them to document last month. They're all the same to Anthony. Bodies to frame. He remains silent on the subject of Colin and devotes one hundred percent of his attention to choosing between two lapel mics, each wound like a shiny worm in its own case. Finally, he snaps one shut, slings the other into his shoulder bag, and pulls down the van's rear door. "Let's get 'er done," he says cheerfully.

They meet Colin at the front door, and Beth is surprised to see that he has changed into a black tank top and a kilt of the kind she's seen footage of him wearing on stage. Under his arm is a leather-bound fiddle case. He says nothing about any of this, so Beth doesn't either. She suggests they take advantage of the morning sun to grab some B-roll on the way down to the dock. They shoot Colin giving a tour of the property. Shoot him standing on the cliff looking out to sea. Shoot him as he walks along the path, lined with flagstone, down to the dock. Beth asks Anthony for specific shots—emblematic shots. A pan from the open sky to Colin's face: the fallen star. A long, slow pull-back from Colin and his instrument to place him on the expanse of land: the lonesome fiddler.

On the dock, which turns out to be very basic, just some boards bound together and bolted to the rock, Colin is restless as Anthony arranges his tripod.

"That thing works, you know," he says, nodding towards the water where a small wooden boat, grey with age, is bobbing. "I could take us out."

"I'm not crazy about going out with the camera," says Anthony, addressing Beth. Even for a cameraman, he is obsessively careful with his equipment. But Colin is literally jumping in place now, and Beth has a sudden vision of Judith playing back the interview they will get on this dock. "Why the hell would you make a manic guy like this stand still? Where's the movement? Where's the MUSIC?" Despite the yelling, Judith is mostly right about TV.

"I wonder if maybe we would be better off out there," Beth says to Anthony, as gently as she's learned she should when overruling him. "If you thought the shot could be steady enough."

"She's good and stable," Colin says about the boat, smiling broadly for the first time.

Anthony looks out into the haze that hovers stubbornly over

the entire shoreline, despite the heat, then over to Colin, as if seeing him for the first time. Beth can tell he puts no stock in the fiddle player's reassurances, that he dislikes how Colin has stepped in to answer her question. A technical question. "It's not about the boat." He turns to Beth. "Just point me to it. I'll get the shot."

With this, he starts walking, Colin trotting after him in his kilt, the two moving rather competitively towards to boat. Beth's experienced this too often to be offended; as the only woman on a shoot she often feels like an afterthought, despite being in charge. She catches up, and Anthony helps her onto the splintered bench that cuts across the triangular prow. He picks up his camera, which he's placed on the dock, and gets in beside her. Colin has already tucked his fiddle case into the boat's flat bottom. Now he loosens the single knot that holds them to the dock and they are adrift on the calm water. He hauls on the ancient-looking motor three times, then sits as it begins to sputter rhythmically, moving them forward. His curly hair ruffles in the breeze. He looks oddly comfortable, like driving a boat is his whole life.

Anthony isn't happy. He has his eye pressed determinedly to his lens, grabbing some shots of this action, his long legs angled high in front of him. Beth realizes she doesn't like the idea of being off land either. The sensory impact of salty air, motor exhaust and the hard seat begins to magnify and she feels dizzy. Her discomfort is only slightly diminished by imagining Judith's face lighting up at the sight of this footage: "MUSICAL!" Beth knows this will work. These images tell the story of the man who got too much too quickly and came back to land where he belongs. A Canadian story. But even as she mentally constructs her winning visual montage, she is conscious of it being only partly true, and her heart sinks as she considers the complexity of even the most mundane life story. This, in turn, stirs an old ache for music; it takes just ten fingertips on a keyboard to handle seemingly endless intricacies.

They putter along parallel to the shore. Colin's house is visible above the cliff. Even the sculptural lightning rod he's mounted on its roof looks authentic. The sea takes on a dreamy quality.

Around the first rocky point, Colin slows the boat and cuts the motor. The water gurgles as it holds and hits the sides. "I fish here," he says. "Good place to start?"

"Yes," says Beth, looking to Anthony, who readies himself wordlessly. She clears her throat. "Maybe I'll begin with a few questions about where we are—"

Colin puts up a hand to indicate that he needs a moment. He reaches into his boot and pulls out a cigarette and a lighter. As he does, the stance of his legs widens abruptly and his kilt lifts high enough to reveal that he has no underwear on. Beth is mute at the sight of his thatch of pubic hair, his penis in retreat against large balls.

"What the hell are you doing?" says Anthony, pulling his eye from the camera.

"Oh, shit," says Colin, putting his knees together and lighting up. "Didn't mean to offend, camera boy. It's not usually so hot here."

Beth has never seen Anthony angry, though she realizes she has come to fear such a moment even more than something happening to his equipment. She is nearly too afraid to look over. When she does, he has returned his eye to the viewer, icily silent.

"Should we start, then?" she says, telling herself it's nothing. An old game Colin has resurrected out of boredom. She's a pro. She can steer this. "Um. Okay. I was wondering if you could talk a little bit about why you live here. And maybe begin by working that question into your answer, so we have a complete statement."

Colin tips his head patronizingly, blowing smoke from his nostrils. Beth blushes. He used to do these kinds of interviews all the time and doesn't need to be told. His abrupt exposure has thrown her.

But not Colin. He now has a lot to say. "I chose to move back to Newfoundland three years ago, near to the day. Wasn't anything for me in the environment where I was spending my time. I still loved music—always loved music. But I realized I didn't want to be where people were making it commercially."

"Do you play locally, then?"

"There aren't many players on this part of the Rock, so I don't play out much," says Colin, looking away vaguely, and Beth feels a glimmer of sympathy for him at the thought that he might be excluded from local jam sessions because of who he is. "But I listen all the time to the water and—" he gestures behind him, then above— "to all this, really. Permanent front-row seat."

Beth looks up to take in the sky, which is very blue beyond the haze. Several gulls are arcing up there, fingernail-sized. The sound they make is distorted, beautifully, by the various drafts of air between them and the water's surface. She has a serene moment thinking that her job takes her so many places, into the worlds of so many people. What a fool she'd have been to give it up for the faint hope of a music career. Doing it full-time could have deafened her, in a way, untethered her from what else is going on in the world. She might have ended up with a narrow focus.

This thought is cut short by Anthony's elbow jabbing her upper arm. He's pulled the camera away again. "Take us back," he says, addressing Colin.

Beth pivots towards Colin. He's widened his knees once more, this time to examine his inner thigh. There are the balls.

"Colin, maybe you would prefer to do the interview in your studio," Beth says.

"No. I'm good," says Colin, winking at Anthony.

"Take us back right now," says Anthony. He has rested his camera across his lap like a dog, one arm cast protectively over its back.

"You don't get to say when we go back to anything," says Colin, waving Anthony's insistence away like a fly.

Beth tries to understand why this is happening, why Colin

has chosen to bait her cameraman, why Anthony is swallowing the lure. "Should we all just take a breath and start over?" she starts to say, but even as she's forming the sentence, Colin is up. The boat, which is surprisingly stable, slips left, then right. She gropes for the side.

"Sit down," says Anthony. "Sit down, start that engine, and take us back."

"I've changed my mind. I don't want to do this. It's not good for me."

The comment feels like an attack, and Beth suspects Colin of lying when he said his record company sprang this interview on him at the last minute. Maybe he was the one who brought them here, caught between a need for people to see him and for them to go away. "You could've told us to leave as soon as we arrived," she says angrily.

"I know," says Colin, and he puts his hands in the air helplessly. "I know." Then he starts to laugh in the most defeated manner Beth can imagine and lets his arms drop to his sides, his cigarette like an eleventh finger pointed downwards with the rest.

In this brief pause, Anthony makes a rapid move, reaching into the bottom of the boat with the free hand that's been draped over his camera and grabs Colin's fiddle case by the handle.

Colin must be medicated. That's what it is, Beth thinks. It's the only explanation for his behaviour so far, for why he doesn't react in time to stop Anthony. A moment too late he reaches for his instrument, dropping his smoke, then looks up from under his brow, which is crinkled with shock. "Give it," he says to Anthony, opening and closing those muscular fingers in front of his face. "Give it."

"Start your engine," says Anthony.

But Colin is already lunging for his fiddle. The boat tips slightly, and the slap-slap of the water against its sides grows uneven. Beth wants to be home. For the first time in many months, she wants her piano, to play until she is calm. But now Anthony dangles the fiddle over the edge of the boat. Colin's priceless fiddle. Irreplaceable. The haze has settled and is all around them, casting a heavy gloom over the moment. Inwardly, Beth forms a command for Anthony to give the fiddle back, but part of her knows it will be useless, that Anthony doesn't take orders from her after all.

The two men tussle and the boat rocks in earnest. Beth knows she has to do something. She stands and steps over the middle bench towards the outboard, gripping the ripcord as soon as she can and yanking on it hard. It comes out far more easily than she's expected, however, and she loses her footing. The back of her knees makes contact with the back corner of the boat. Suddenly, she is underwater. Every inch of her body is frazzled by the unexpected cold, inducing severe nausea. She has successfully started the engine, and now it comes within an inch of her face, tossing bubbles into her eyes and nostrils and causing her to gasp and take in a mouthful of supersaturated salt water. For no sane reason she recalls the lyrics to the very first song she ever wrote, at fifteen. The song, which was quite terrible, began, "How do you know when you're really through? When you've sunk too low to swim the blue?" She could laugh at the corny resonance, and this helps delay her panic. She expects an arm, probably Anthony's, to pull her up any moment. None does. Then, alone, her lungs bursting, suddenly frantic, she tears at the water with her hands, kicking the ocean beneath her as if it were an assailant, and makes her way to the surface. Looking around, coughing, she spots the boat doubling back, the two men seated like cutout figures. Colin kills the engine and they drift close. Anthony helps her back over the side. Beth throws up on her clothes and lies like a caught fish, curled at the bottom between them.

In silence, they return to shore and unpack themselves, the fiddle, and the camera gear. Beth has lost a shoe. She removes the other and walks up to the house, not stopping until she has ascended the stairs and located Colin's bathroom, where she strips and takes a shower. Afterwards, as she wraps herself in a towel,

Colin's voice comes through the door. "I'm leaving clothes and some flip-flops. We're downstairs."

Ten minutes later, Beth descends towards the kitchen in the too-big sandals and clothes that smell cottony and provoke an unwelcome feeling of gratitude towards Colin, whom she can hear talking. She finds him and Anthony making lunch. Bacon is frying. A large bowl of blueberries has been set on the table. They both turn to her with beseeching looks. Unable to face them, she escapes down the hall, finding herself at the door near Émile Benoît, who now looks to Beth less sleepy than like someone entirely in his place and time. Anthony approaches cautiously and places his hand on her shoulder, but she bends away. She orders him to the studio to set up. They'll do the interview as planned. She walks to the kitchen and, refusing the omelet Colin has prepared, tells him she wants to see the fiddle again. It should be in the shot. He doesn't object.

He's also changed clothes, wears a check shirt that nearly matches the one he's lent Beth. In the studio Anthony rigs it with the lapel mic he chose earlier. Colin doesn't sulk or bait. The sit-down goes exactly as Beth originally imagined it. Colin offers no new information about his past. When Beth asks whether he can see himself going back to music in the future, say ten years from now, he says no, adding, "It's not the time for music. I'm getting into carpentry."

The comment instantly brings Judith to mind, her face downcast at the poor record Beth has managed of this day, at the inevitable demise of her show. When the first thirty-minute tape is full, Anthony and Colin both shift a little, each with an air of relief.

"I'm not done," says Beth, handing Anthony another blank tape. He hesitates. In TV it's considered unwise to record more than you need. You can get lost in all the raw images. Beth licks her lips, still salty, then turns away from him and back to Colin, whose fingers are flexing nervously, seeing that Beth has a lot more to ask.

THAT OBSCURE DESIRE

David is preparing to meet a woman, something he doesn't do often because he works long hours, because he hates rejection and so doesn't ask many out, and, most importantly, because even though he inhabits a world of glamorous people, he isn't one. He is extremely self-conscious and, even now, at age thirty, at his very peak, when he should be benefiting fully from lifelong privilege and his own salary, he fears dates and has to do facial exercises in his bathroom mirror beforehand in order to loosen his expression away from one he does not intend, which looks like antagonistic surprise.

It makes sense that Stéphanie is the woman he's meeting. She's half French, half Canadian farm child, from a ranch in a part of that country David had never heard of before, Manitoba. She is not even a bit Mexican, like he is, and from a different (lower) social class. She can't place him, then, can't tell how people on his home turf see him. This is why he has risked suggesting a date. He doesn't need to know much about her. He has surmised that whatever world she comes from is productive of university-educated language teachers who live abroad more cheaply than they can at home, riding the elevators of government law offices like the one where he works, wearing inappropriately casual clothes, with a manner and a walk that exude sexual confidence and eagerness to accept the attention they get just for being from somewhere else—none of which bothers him in the least.

The first day of their new mandatory French classes, David and several colleagues watched Stéphanie enter the conference room. She was nervous and excited the way people are when they are forced to parade past many others who have nowhere else to look. David guessed that all the men judged her the way he did: as tall, with high, firm breasts, but also imperfectly proportioned, with long legs and a too-short torso. The women probably focused on the hair (curly and gathered into a high knot), the skin (whiter than any in the room, marked by former acne), and the clothes (a beige V-neck sweater and straight black pants). She pulled herself up onto the front desk, briskly crossed her legs, and turned on a flat, forward-reaching smile in which David, who enjoyed watching her move, who knew he wouldn't be judged for staring, saw the marks of a practical nature that could handle pressure. This toughness drew him in and gave him pause to consider how it might feel to hold those long legs in his hands.

"*Bonsoir, je m'appelle Stéphanie*," was how she began a short autobiographical speech that described, in a voice that was edgy, confessional, and self-assured, her French blood, rural upbringing, passion for travel, and choice of Mexico City against the protests of her parents and her very-recently-no-longer boyfriend. This last bit of gossip brought chuckles from those who knew more French than David. But Stéphanie was democratic. She frowned at the two-tiered reception, repeated her speech in Spanish, ex-boyfriend comment and all, and nipped in the bud the prospect of inside jokes between her and the bilingual minority (whose parents had probably already sent them to Paris for tutoring), and let everyone else, including David, laugh too.

As the weeks have come and gone and he's grown to understand more of Stéphanie's French words and her jokes, finding them all quite funny—so different from the stale chitchat of the women in his office, who have all been brought up to hate one other, and who nearly all married young and are involved in the kinds of affairs he both despises and also dreams of carrying on himself if he were married—David has found that all of Stéphanie's mannerisms evoke the same desire in him to take hold of some part of her body. Over this time, to his delight, the other men in the class, impatient with the new language requirement (based on their department's *sociedad* with the French government) and so disposed to want to flee anyway, have relegated Stéphanie to the status of furniture—she's there, she's useful, she's fine, but not beautiful or well-packaged enough to stand out the way a piece of art does. She isn't Parisian, after all; she was raised alongside cattle. Keeping pace with their disinterest, the women, submissive, always, to groupthink, have also let Stéphanie drop from their well-calibrated radars. She is neither a source of envy nor a threat.

Invisible then, and so reduced, at least in her working hours, to something resembling his own low rank among his peers, Stéphanie has come to occupy a heightened presence in David's consciousness. Her low-heeled shoe stepping off the elevator, her arm raised against her portable blackboard, the too-soft "rrr"s when she speaks to them in Spanish—these details have affected him with cumulative force, resulting, last week, about four months into their acquaintance, in his waking up one morning, staring out the bedroom window at the workers reinforcing the high white fence outside his apartment building, and surprising himself by thinking, There are too many barriers in my life, then saying aloud, "I'll ask Stéphanie out."

He could not wait long to carry out his mission. He needed to capitalize on the way his passion seemed to be running ahead of his fear. That same evening, after his lesson, he forced himself to linger as the rest of his colleagues filed out of French class reaching for car keys, discussing their weekend plans for Acapulco, Cuernavaca, and other hot spots within driving distance of the city. He stepped towards her. She was stacking her papers neatly on the front desk. "Mlle. Stéphanie."

"*Sí, David?*" She looked up with the smile he'd seen her use many times with other students.

His enthusiasm waned a bit at the generic reception, one that seems to greet him wherever he goes, like the half-hearted tail wag of an old dog. He pressed on. "Have you been to the *Cineteca*?" he asked in English, thinking that in this third language they would both speak with the same limitation of an accent. "Because they have really very good movies on weekends there— not Hollywood. Artistic films."

"Oh?" said Stéphanie, changing her expression, truly seeing

him for the first time, doing a scan of his face, looking, he thought, for something interesting, something to convince her to accept his offer. "I didn't know about it. I usually go to the regular place on Insurgentes," she replied, and her English sounded perfect.

David became nervous. "Yes. That's fine. I'm not against Hollywood films."

"You're not? Well, you should be. They mostly suck."

"Yes, they do. I just meant, since you're American…"

"*French*-Canadian. Not everyone north of the border is the same." She shook her head like she had run into this blurring of national identities before.

"No, I know. I didn't mean…" David stumbled, feeling his passion slowing in the race against resentment, sensing Stéphanie's amusement at his discomfort. He remembered so many social occasions in his life when he'd been mocked. Still, he tried to believe that there might be room, in this case, to gain better footing. "It's—you seem to understand all these cultures—ours, French, American, Canadian. You might appreciate a foreign film more than most."

"Well, thank you, David. So… are you inviting me?"

"Sorry, yes. Friday?"

"Friday would be fine. I could do Friday at the movies, sure."

Between that brief exchange and now, as David steps into the security of the *sitio* taxi that will take him to Stéphanie's neighbourhood (he does not trust hailed cabs with all of the robberies), his mind has swirled, storm-like, with painful hope. Speaking to his mother yesterday, competing as always for her attention against the staff and the dramas of her gallery in the south end, he mentioned an upcoming evening with a foreigner. To his satisfaction, his mother became fully focused on him. She later commented that she hoped this *canadiense* (said with a note of derision) was "good enough for you"—which he knew to interpret as "rich enough." He was aware that in person his mother would find Stéphanie artless, that his father—whose girlfriend was a TV hostess who had undergone more than one surgery to her face in the past years, evolving it towards extreme symmetry—would recognize in Stéphanie yet more proof that his son could not compete. Tapping into a vein of masochism, David smiled to himself as he envisioned an event in the near future (a dinner? a day trip to Taxco?) that would force his parents into his and Stéphanie's charmless company, how this would place the cold truth of his parents' respective characters on display, out past their veneer of sophistication, which they have always blamed him for not cultivating.

The first thing he notices, meeting Stéphanie at the café they've agreed on, is that she looks no different than she does in class. Relaxed, completely at ease (too much so?) and wearing another version of her typically neutral sweater-and-pant combination, she could be about to discuss the *passé composé*, has gone through none of the trouble that a Friday night out with a man calls for. From the moment they sit down, she talks incessantly about her Condesa apartment, her new friends, her difficult adjustment to Mexican food. David is quickly annoyed, having presumed that she would be more interested in what he had to say, in *his* insights into Mexico, a city he loves for its contradictions, for its ability to hold within it the lives of nine million people as different as those of his parents and the beggars who, just then, pass the outer fence of the café terrace, their dirty, cracked palms wide open.

"This movie sounds very good," says Stéphanie, smiling her flat smile.

"Yes. You know, Buñuel lived in Mexico City and made a lot of films here. It was so much less dangerous then."

"To tell you the truth, David, I'm actually kind of sick of hearing people talk about how dangerous it is here. I am not going to live in fear. I didn't move here to become a prisoner of some snobby neighbourhood."

David isn't sure how to respond. While he is from this city and she is the visitor, somehow it seems like the other way around.

Stéphanie lifts her hand to get the waiter's attention. When he comes over, she asks him for another coffee, handing him her cup. "It's not hot," she says.

David tries to understand what kind of experience of Mexico Stéphanie has come for. Is it this kind of neighbourhood, where guards are placed in front of every bar and restaurant? Or for permission to behave like she owns the place? He worries about her reason for accepting his offer of a date. If she has come to dominate others, how far down the ladder of power has she placed him?

After coffee Stéphanie says she'd enjoy riding the subway to the film and, though with the exception of some teenaged escapes from his private school to cantinas in the *Centro*, he has rarely ventured into the cavernous, dense-with-use underground, David agrees, having become discombobulated at the café and not wanting to seem like one of the snobs she's referred to. On the train, as they sway in their uncomfortable orange plastic seats, Stéphanie tells him that she learned the value of money in her early teens by raising her own pigs, the profits used to help fund her university education. David smiles and shakes his head, assuming that she has invented this tale to test him humorously, as David once tested a Belgian client by claiming that he and his colleagues stored their ponchos and guns in their cars. But Stéphanie's face hardens and David's laugh comes off as cruel: There was no test, but somehow he has still managed to fail.

Stéphanie quickly changes the subject to her work, for which she is being grossly underpaid, she believes, by a boss who snorts away his gross earnings. David is careful not to react positively or negatively to the mention of drug use, unable to guess whether Stéphanie is morally opposed to it or whether she just dislikes her boss. Since the pig-raising discussion, he understands that knowing next to nothing about his date will likely work against him. Stéphanie goes on, adding that she is considering trying her hand at modelling. She hears it's easy to find that kind of work in

Mexico, even for women who wouldn't have a chance at home. She points a thumb at herself and rolls her eyes. Again, David doesn't react immediately, unsure whether to protest or agree, knowing that what she says is true. He decides to lie. "Well, I'm sure they would take you regardless."

She lets out a short, bitter laugh, but thanks him. Meanwhile, David asks himself why he continues to feel so uncomfortable, why Stéphanie's humour, her manner, her *campo* life experience, her poor Spanish grammar (she keeps misusing the past tense, confusing things she's done with things she does habitually) are making him wish he were home now, reading or surfing online, rather than riding the subway with this foreigner and subject to the alternatively suspicious, envious, fascinated and angry stares of the dark working people all around them.

A few stops into the ride, two musicians dressed in thinning country clothes board the subway car just as David has finally begun his own story about a particularly unpleasant and corrupt bureaucrat he has to deal with at work. The musicians strum determinedly at their homemade instruments, and while most passengers remain impassive at their warbling falsettos "...*Yo sé perder, yo sé perder...*", Stéphanie is obviously moved, and David, unable to sustain any momentum, drops his story to listen with her. "They make so much from what they have," Stéphanie whispers. David makes eye contact with one of the musicians, who has the look of a criminal, and feels a wave of disgust for the city's poor, the likes of which has not gripped him in a long while. "*Quiero volver, volver, volver...*" continue the singers.

At the film, they find two good seats and watch as the dated, unnaturally deep green palm trees of the opening shot of *That Obscure Object of Desire* replace the darkness. Halfway through the film, when the character of the maid, Conchita, exposes her breasts, David loses himself in thoughts of sex with Stéphanie and excuses himself to go to the bathroom where, without having planned to do so, he masturbates in haste. When he returns to his seat Stéphanie leans towards him and asks with concern, "Was everything all right in there?" He nods and they turn to face the screen in time to witness the cruel humiliation of the male lead at the gate of the house he's bought for his young mistress. Stéphanie leans forward, deeper into the film's flicker, enthralled.

Afterwards, David insists that they take a taxi back to her apartment, as he cannot bring himself to ride the dreaded subway again. Stéphanie agrees, but before David can dig for his cell phone to call his regular cab company, she hails one of the hundreds of green-and-white Volkswagen Beetles that stream past on the busy street fronting the Cineteca. One comes to a stop and Stéphanie bends to crawl inside. David opens his mouth to protest but hesitates. He has noticed Stéphanie's long left leg, held behind her in a way that makes him want to follow. Pausing a moment to squint at the driver's ID, which is posted on the passenger's side window, David finds it looks authentic enough and gets in, snapping the door shut behind him.

"Condesa, *por favor*," he says. The driver does not respond. He pulls them quickly into traffic. David looks at Stéphanie, who is staring out her window at the passing city—crumbling overpasses, steam rising from dimly lit, all-night food stands, graffitied walls—while humming the song they heard on the subway. David is aware that, according to her logic, he is the opposite of the musicians, a bad Mexican, with so much at his disposal and doing so little with it. At the same time, he is equally aware of the closeness of her body, the smell of her curly hair, which she wears down tonight—maybe her only concession to getting dressed up—and so close his knuckles might brush the ends. Her clean smell mixes with the night air coming through the driver's open window and the persistent metallic undertone of pollution. Stéphanie turns his way, gives him a long look and smiles a smile he does not recognize from any previous conversations. It seems content, which is enough to reignite his hope and to let him forgive her selfish, inattentive behaviour. This is a date after all; she is not to be added to his roster of women friends. Stéphanie opens her mouth to say something. David leans closer.

But at the same moment, the driver brakes, jerking the car to the side of the highway and to a sudden stop, causing both passengers to come sharply forward then back against their seats like rag dolls. "What the hell is going on?" says David, his heart thumping frantically as it dawns on him exactly what is happening. The doors open, the driver steps calmly out and two men jump in, one through each door, twin handguns poised at the level of the front-seat headrests. "Shut your eyes," yells one, then the other. "Shut your fucking eyes." But now David cannot tell who says what because, doing as he is told, his eyelids are squeezed hard together. "Keep them shut and put your head down on your lap or we'll shoot you dead right here."

"Go!" says one of the men, and the car jerks into motion.

"Everything you have, *pendejos*. Quickly. Everything. Keep your head down and your fucking eyes closed."

David hears Stéphanie fumble for her purse and jewelry. He pulls out his wallet and cell phone. He removes his single ring and the watch his father gave him for finishing law school. In the void of his closed eyes, time slows considerably and, in his fear, he grows distant from his body, from the threats of the men in the front seat, far, even, from the smell of Stéphanie's hair. He sees again his graduation ceremony, his parents sitting uncomfortably side by side looking strained, bored and hot, while around him female classmates natter and the men speak in low tones, testing out the casual arrogance of grownups. He sees, too, as though from a third eye, or from the perspective of someone like Stéphanie, himself, not short, not ugly, but not at all remarkable, set apart from the rest, graduating into a career and a life that he already knows will never lead to freedom and will be outlasted by the Mexican sun and even by the pollution that, for the length of his graduation ceremony, almost entirely obscured it.

The robbers take all the things David holds out to them then demand that he hand over his loafers too. They hurl insults at their captives. They make lewd comments about the *blanca*, the *gringa* who, David notices, makes hardly a sound. David momentarily considers some kind of chivalrous protest, but something hard and cool pushes against his forehead. Instinctively, he opens his eyes.

There, pressed to his thin skin, is a gun; behind it, a curled, chapped hand, jittering; behind it, the *ladrón* himself, a teenager who looks angry, but also interested, like he's busy figuring out who he's holding up, filing David into his own preconceived categories of Mexicans with too much. "Close your eyes, you *fraisa* motherfucker, while I shoot you like a dog!"

But now David can't do as he's told. He's stuck, wants to know exactly how he is being seen through this stranger's eyes, just as, he realizes, he has craved to know himself through Stéphanie's. The teenager's hand shakes behind the gun, but its end remains firmly against David's forehead. "Close them! Close them!" he repeats. David's eyes remain wide open.

"*Vamos*, Pedro. *Vamos!*" says the other man.

"Close your eyes, you *fraisa*, you *pinche puto*. Close your eyes."

"David. Do what he says," says Stéphanie, surprising them all with a calm voice. "Do it."

And David does. A moment later, he hears the car doors open. The men get out as someone gets in. The doors snap shut again. A voice says, "What address in Condesa?" David slowly opens his eyes to find the original driver back in his seat, pulling them into the busy stream of traffic.

"Get out," says the driver when they arrive at Stéphanie's apartment building. They obey. As his toes meet the cool pavement through his socks, David remembers that he has no shoes, no wallet, no keys, no money. He walks forward like a beggar.

"My roommate can buzz us in. Come on," says Stéphanie, taking his arm and leading him towards the door of a decaying art deco building typical of the neighbourhood.

Upstairs they file past the roommate with a quiet hello from Stéphanie and proceed immediately to her room where, without breaking step or turning on any lights, Stéphanie collapses onto her bed with a long sigh. David closes the door, follows her, and sits down on the edge of the bed. He looks out through the steel bars covering her floor-to-ceiling bedroom window and down the three stories of the building to the near-empty street below, illuminated by streetlights. He notices how some thick branches of bougainvillea on a neighbour's balcony—its flowers so perfectly translucent with colour in the afternoon sun—have turned a deep blood red in this light. They are dark, still, and gathered as though for protection.

"I was going to tell you…" says Stéphanie quietly, lying on her back.

"What?" he says, permitting himself to fall back and lie beside her, pointing his eyes at the high ceiling.

"Earlier tonight, before… I was going to tell you," she repeats, in a near whisper. "I've gotten back together with my boyfriend. He's supposed to come here soon, to visit."

"I see."

David lets his head turn away from Stéphanie towards her night table, noticing, as he does, that the bedroom is almost completely bare except for a photo of her parents taped up near the window, two art posters and some novels stacked at the foot of the bed. He thinks, again, of what explains Stéphanie's presence here, out of her country, away from her people. He wonders about her farm life and ethnic mix, and how these things express themselves in everything—her clothes, her accent, her desire to pretend she is safe. He feels pity, but not for her. He turns his whole body her way as she lies very straight and with her eyes tightly closed, as though she's still carrying out the orders of the men in the taxi. Then David reaches an arm over her and moves his forehead to touch her hair. The pity ebbs before he can name its object. In its place comes a present-tense interest in touch.

TORERA

She steps off the bus and makes her way to the side, where the young driver has already opened the hinged horizontal door and is rapidly extracting people's luggage. When he sees her, he stops what he's doing, skips over some other waiting passengers, and hurries to her side. She points at her backpack. The driver nods like it will be his great pleasure to follow her finger and enters the rippled metal compartment with more than the necessary masculine crouching and reaching. He stands the backpack between them, fingering the tag. A few steps off, an older couple in matching, unseasonably thick black cardigans mumble and raise their hands in what must be European gestures of annoyance. The driver ignores them. "Heer you go, Seyr—eed—en from Canada."

"Sheridan."

The driver smiles warmly. "Sheyree-*dahn*. I should know. Pardon my English. Is—"

"No. You shouldn't know."

The day is hot. The other passengers have arranged themselves in a staggered row and are staring over one another's shoulders. The driver wishes them away with his turned back, speaks in a leisurely fashion, one hand resting on the bag. "In Canada is normal name, yes?"

"No. Nowhere. Anyway. I'll take that." She pulls the bag roughly towards herself, leaving his hand pressing the air.

The driver looks dismayed but shrugs it off, retracting his flirtation like it is the collapsible handle of one of the wheeled suitcases he now moves towards.

Sheridan hoists the pack onto her shoulder and walks off, ignoring the ripple of dirty looks following her. She is not ashamed of cutting ahead or of her abruptness towards the driver. Quite the opposite. Here, a full continent from Janet, the woman who stuck her with such a moronic name, she is under no obligation to consider people's feelings. There is no Sheridan or Sheyree-dahn. No daughter or unwilling sister-to-be. She'll be Sheri, traveller, stranger.

Sheri plods upwards along the cobblestone road that leads into the town, which sits like a jumble of cubes at the very top of a hill overlooking the Mediterranean. She is surprised at how run-down the place looks up close. Whitewashed medieval houses are interspersed with garbage-strewn empty lots, bricks disintegrating into red dust over candy wrappers and empty water bottles. The commercial zone is dominated by shops selling racks of plastic bulls, overly elaborate sunhats, flamenco dolls. The dolls wear heavy makeup, with saccharine expressions of pinched red lips and thick eyelashes like hairy spiders. They make Sheri think of Janet. Stopping at the least offensive establishment in sight, Sheri gives in to a sudden, pressing need for a drink.

Inside it is as achingly hot as on the street. Compact, dirty electronic lottery terminals bleat out little noises to her right. She heads to the bar, where only men are standing, where the smoke is thick, and sets her pack down with a thud.

"*Díme*," says the server, a short man Sheri judges as typically southern Spanish. This opinion is based on nothing; she is on her first trip outside Canada.

Sheri stares at him, not understanding. She feels the eyes of the men come over her like a rash. She rolls her own towards the ceiling. Besides her name, her looks are her greatest albatross. She is 'hot' in exactly the way she despises in her mother: like a naughty catalogue model, or a wholesome peeler in her off hours. She can add plastic flamenco twit to that list now. Sheri has tried to beat back the Janet genes, has kept her hair short, hidden her body, earned her Master's in library science. But she's never totally shaken a sexiness that makes men equal parts eager to please and angry.

"*Cerveza*," she says, and the server fills an ancient, water-spotted pint glass until it froths over the lip. Sheri takes a long, cool drink. Alcohol is a reliable means of reducing her unease. The jet lag must be kicking in, though, because after downing half the pint she feels just as exposed. Her stubborn sobriety combines with disappointment in her surroundings to create a sense of doom. Sheri realizes that she is already lonely. It's partly her own fault. She has never really wanted to travel. For her, knowing a place well feels like the point of being an adult. She has mapped and remapped Toronto over her lifetime, and the work of rediscovering it at each new age does not bore her. In a way, leaving it has been a betrayal, like walking away from a friend halfway through a conversation. She should've stayed put.

Another cool sip of beer. No. It was impossible with Janet there. Being that rare kind of neglectful parent that never leaves you alone long enough to enjoy it, Janet has booby-trapped Sheri's home city, showing up when she shouldn't, calling at odd hours with surprise information. Sheri had to get out.

"Hello," says a voice on Sheri's left, and she turns sharply, prepared to project hostility. When she does, she sees that it is a much older man. At least fifty. Tall as a basketball player but no muscle. She thinks of a stick bug, but with a dwindling patch of faded, strawberry-blonde hair. He brings up a greasy, half-empty beer glass, his bony elbow triangulating out, then salutes her. "American, are ya?" he says, and to Sheri he sounds like industrial-era England.

"Canadian."

"Ah. The colonies. Wonderful." The man is an idiot and a drunk. Sheri looks around and considers her options for company. The other men, none clearly English-speaking, have all returned to staring into their brews.

"Here for the sun, are y—?" he begins to ask, but Sheri's cell phone rings inside her backpack.

"Excuse me," she says, and steps outside.

"It's working," says Janet, when Sheri answers. "I wondered."

"What."

"Just checking that you're wherever it is you decided to go."

"I'm turning this off."

"If you do, I'll call your boss and tell him you're not coming back—to cancel your leave and fill your spot at the research desk. You know I would."

Sheri says nothing. Janet is not happy with the trip either. Predictably, this has made her trigger-happy with her threats. Sheri pictures her mother falling into the gaping mouth of a volcano.

"I'm huge," says Janet, sighing, moving on. "Just this past day, I got bigger. Your brother's going to be a bruiser. It's what Roger wanted."

"I'm hanging up."

"Sheridan."

"What."

"Just enjoy yourself. Make it worth it. Missing the birth, I mean. Suck the marrow out of your little adventure."

What made such a woman? Sheri considers this question as she stands with her closed phone, regretting bringing it. Her only theory is that it was her own appearance, as a fetus in Janet's teenaged womb, that ruined her mother. Sheri can almost feel guilty over it. But then, there's her name. Borrowed from a character on daytime television, yanked off like a shabby wig and plunked down on her before she could argue. It was so unnecessary. Pathetic, really. "Sheridan" was Janet's way of defying her own diminished prospects. The name superimposed soap opera drama over her real life like a coloured transparency. It was not a wish for her future child but for Janet herself—one that never came true, of course. Janet's life has amounted to a series of laborious attempts to get things from men, with Sheri along for the ride. Just as Sheri felt, at age thirty-one, that she was nearly free from Janet's grip, her mother produced another twist: at age forty-five, she has invested a large amount of her third husband's money to enlist medical science in making her pregnant with her second child, due any day.

Back inside, the tall man is standing with his back to the bar. He looks like a giraffe in faded denims. Sheri feels her heart defrosting. She comes to stand beside him. "I'm running away," she says.

He nods meaningfully. "Good place ta do it. Cheap drink. Excellent ham."

Two beers later, Sheri has heard the bulk of Andy's—that's his name—unhappy life story, and she has told him hers. She thinks hers is worse but doesn't say so. She enjoys how Andy undercuts serious subjects like bad mothers and British divorce law with non sequiturs, randomly inserting information he has gathered about Moorish history, Spain's drought, and the population of snails that clings to the town's stucco walls. Factual things that make Sheri feel less unhinged, like the gravity she experiences searching databases.

And she was wrong: Andy's a drinker, but he's not stupid. He asks good questions, listens carefully as Sheri provides more self-description. She hears herself tell him that she is "not very adventurous," that she is "terrible with children," that she would not like to "be stuck raising some little brother" she never asked for, which, she adds, she could easily see happening, knowing Janet. To all of this Andy nods, his upper lip permanently fuzzy with foam. She realizes that even if he was the only man left on earth, she would not sleep with him. Sheri, traveller, stranger, needs companions, not lovers. She needs distance, to have others judge her as the person she intends to become. Independent. Not at all shabby.

Still, having made no plans besides being here, she agrees to meet him at the beach the next day. Sheri then checks in at the *pensión* she booked online. Her goal is to sleep away the day, but the *pensión* turns out to be the back bedroom of an old woman's house, itself a set of confining rooms with cracked marble floors, plentiful doilies, closed curtains and heavy, dark brown furniture. The owner speaks no English. With enthusiastic smiling and use of her hands, however, she lets Sheri know that she would like to make her supper in exchange for an extra twenty euros. Sheri shakes her head while backing away, looking for the bathroom. No sooner has she relieved herself than the woman returns, knocking continuously until Sheri opens. Janet is exactly like this. She has never been able to respect Sheri's privacy, which robs Janet of her only consistent audience.

Opening the door, Sheri exudes coldness. "What?" The woman only grins again, hands her a thin towel and bar of green soap. Sheri closes the door, turns on the water, sits in the bathtub, and tries to maneuver the hand-held shower head. The foreignness of everything—the woman's extremely scented soap, the echo of the low-pressured water running down the drain—returns a rising panic. As soon as she's finished, Sheri asks the woman for the phone and pulls out a bar napkin from her back pocket. "Andy? Hi. It's Sheri. Yeah. Could we go swimming? Now?"

An hour later Sheri has descended from the town, past another newer and uglier commercial strip, and is walking along the beach in the direction that Andy has told her to go. Though she loves to swim, she has never liked beaches. This one does not look promising. There are rocky areas at the water's edge that resemble shelves of lava rock. The sand is pebbly. Not as fine as the pictures online suggested, nor even as the sands of Lake Huron, where Janet's newest husband, Roger, has a monster cottage and where Janet required Sheri to spend last July 1st weekend in exchange for vowing not to call except on Sundays. Janet broke the pact five days later with news of her pregnancy. Sheri breathes hard with effort as her sandals sink into the sand over and over, the grains running through her toes. She scans all the cheap white beach chairs she passes. Eventually, on the outer edge of one row, someone in a skinny Speedo waves. Sheri stops cold at the sight. Even from where she's standing, the details of Andy's legs, his elongated torso and arms, his encased penis, are prominent. The praying mantis on vacation. Sheri feels she will either turn and run or laugh out loud. She forces herself to keep going.

"Whur's the suit?" Andy deadpans as she approaches.

Sheri smiles. Under her T-shirt and shorts she's got on the same one-piece she wears to the YMCA back in Canada. "It's here. Nothing to write home about."

Andy gets up and bends over to reach into his bag. Sheri marvels at his rear, which is so slight that the Speedo, with nothing to cling to, hangs forlornly from his hipbones. "Back in a jiff," he says, closing a fist on some coloured euros and striding towards a café behind them.

Andy returns a few minutes later with two iced drinks, each with a decorative umbrella. "For what ails ya," he says, toasting Sheri, who has stripped to her bathing suit and taken the chair next to his.

They talk as they did earlier. Sheri tells him more about her life. How she came into the world because her mother didn't want to bother the married man she was sleeping with to wear a condom—not that Janet was so into that guy. He was just her fifteen-year-old's ticket out of her own mother's house. And into sex. Janet developed early and was curious, apparently. Also, she claims there was some kind of funny business going on at the time between her and her mother, who also hit her. But Sheri, who spent years of her life around her grandmother, has her doubts about this claim. Janet has a tendency to make herself the distressed heroine of all her relationships. When Andy asks how Sheri knows so much, she explains that Janet has repeated these things to her a thousand times. "Her life is like a porn magazine she leaves lying around. The only shock is that anyone actually believes her bullshit. Like Roger."

"Maybe he luvs 'er."

Sheri guffaws. "Loves! Do you know what she told me the day she found out that the fertility treatment had worked? She said, "'I'll beat Demi Moore by a year.' Christ. That's probably all it's about for her."

"For 'er. Okay. But 'im?"

Sheri gets up. "You want another?" she says, exasperated.

Andy smiles. "Won't stop ya."

Several more drinks, and Andy decides it's time for their swim. They get up and trot across the hot sand. Sheri is quite tipsy and has some trouble on the lava-like rocks. She generally embraces her drinking, but the librarian in her doesn't approve of the attendant loss of focus. Each time she finds herself impaired, becoming clumsy or slurring, there's a moment when she exits her body and watches from the point of view of someone in far greater control. That person always says the same thing: "It's so boring." One solution is to drink more. When that is not possible, as it is not now, Sheri must concentrate to return her feelings of self-worth.

Andy gives her his hand so she won't fall. His grip is stronger than she expected, pleasingly so. Finally, Sheri lets herself into the water and paddles out. "I've never been in the ocean before," she says, but Andy has already dived down. He emerges a moment later quite a bit further away, his red-skinned, matt-haired head like a bobber. He waves for her to join him and they make their way beyond the break, where they tread water side by side in the swells. "It's like the womb," says Andy, tilting his head back so that his hair floats on the surface. The comment makes Sheri laugh, but then she stops, wondering if he's making fun of her. "Not for me," she says with the same sharpness she used with the bus driver. "I'm planning to get my tubes tied." She has never said this aloud before, but she's known it for a long time. Still, the sound of the words, tossed back at her by the water, is a rebuke. It repels her.

Sheri begins front crawling towards shore. The harder she swims, however, the less progress she makes. Some kind of cross current is working against her. The sun feels like it's burning into her skull and she is frantic to be on shore. Sheri crawls and crawls.

Andy comes close with what seem like a few easy strokes. "Everything okay?"

Sheri nods, unable to speak from exertion, and keeps going. By the time she can touch ground, she is too tired to stand and has to work her way back over the lava rocks using her hands. "I'm in bad shape," she says, panting.

Andy helps her stand. "Time to head out, I'd say."

He walks her to their chairs, where they gather their things and go further up the beach to a wooden shack that serves as a change room. Inside, they are bathed in shadow, in stagnant air.

Sheri feels like crying. Instead, she presses herself against Andy's long torso. He says nothing, and she is grateful not to be checked, or forced to think any further. Sheri has had very few lovers. Andy is older than any of them, taller. Miraculously, he manages to get inside her from their standing position. He is not overly zealous. She realizes that this has been the core appeal of all the men she's been with. But now she is thinking, and she understands that her actions are no better than Janet's—evasion through men and sex. The shabbiness of this strategy pervades the moment. Sheri looks around at the damp wooden walls, where blue paint has peeled away, and down at the poured cement floor, where one of her dirty sandals lies upside down.

"Please stop," she says.

Andy halts. Still leaning against her, breathing irregularly, he pulls up his Speedo.

"I—"

"No need. Wur both tired." He bends down to slap a bug from his leg and Sheri misses his next statement.

"Sorry?" she asks.

Andy stands straight. His eyes are warm, bloodshot. "I said, yar gonna hafta come to tha bullfights. It's a must."

Four days later, Andy leads with a pointy kneecap, the bones practically visible under the meager flesh of his legs, which have been left mostly uncovered by short tan shorts. He's edging past the last of several people they've had to cross to reach their seats inside the old stone stadium the next town over. "Top bill is a big-deal celebrity aroun' here, 'lright?" says Andy, sitting heavily, then opening a faded leather satchel and pulling out two bottles of wine, sandwiches, a box of pastries. "Show-off, though. He'll hafta watch's family jew'ls."

Sheri lathers up with sunblock and feels excited, imagining the imminent showdown between man and beast.

Andy picks up the box of pastries and turns in his seat to present it to a woman behind them. The woman, whose makeup is theatrical and whose hair is drawn into a topknot decorated with red, crisscrossed piping, smiles and takes two, then holds out a bag of what look like homemade doughnuts. Sheri is nearly too culture-shocked to reach in, but overrides it. She brings one of the long, thin doughnuts to her mouth. "*Churros*," the woman says, patting Sheri on the shoulder and nodding. "*Churros.*"

Andy explains some of the facts of bullfighting, emphasizing the bravery of the *torero*. Sheri listens to him with the attention she has come to enjoy providing during his bouts of informative talk. Though they have seen each other every day since they met, they have not revisited the beach encounter. Whenever Sheri recalls the moment, she startles. Alone at her *pensión*, she has sat on her hard single bed, trying to take the startle apart and determine how she feels about Andy as a romantic interest. She knows she experiences at least surprise for chucking her traveller-stranger persona moments after she conceived it, but also regret for assuming the worst of herself. There's relief in there too, because now that she has touched Andy and he has touched her, they are at ease, like they've known each other a long time, and this has displaced her loneliness, at least for now.

More people have made their way into the stands. A buzz of anticipation has built all around them. Some groups of people sing songs. Others simply stare down into the ring impatiently. Finally, a bugle sounds and great commotion begins as a parade of men, some riding horses fitted with heavy, gleaming armour, enter the ring.

"The *paseíllo*," says Andy, as the matadors and their teams stroll around the dirt ring, waving at a balcony where several local dignitaries are seated. Andy points out the lead matador, and Sheri is thrilled by the sight of his gilded costume and knee socks. The library recently catalogued a coffee table book depicting Spain in the early 20th century, and it's like seeing that past brought to life. But as the matador continues to circle, Sheri becomes progressively more suspicious. He prances forward with such plain vanity, such satisfaction with his own tight-bottomed form, that she can only think of her mother arriving for a visit in one of her fitted designer maternity outfits.

"He's dedicatin' the fight t' the wife," says Andy, nodding towards the spot, ringside, where a woman with a small child against her shoulder is grinning as the matador waves his hat in her direction.

A moment later a bull is released, roaring through the wooden gate, all muscle, huge at the front, bucking and snuffling like a cartoon. Sheri is moved by its rough beauty. The matador's team goes through a protracted series of moves, each of which involves sticking something sharp into its back, often from horseback. "It's just to calm 'm down," Andy explains.

Sheri, who is starting to understand that bullfights are stacked heavily in favour of the human participants, does not agree that stabbing is calming. She looks towards Andy, but he is attending to the spectacle with the same lack of zealousness he has shown her before. Sheri turns from him, away from the blood running down the bull's side, too, and sees the matador's wife across the way, smiling at her runt like it's the best thing she's ever seen. Their intimacy gives Sheri a familiar pang, and she feels she has nowhere else to turn.

But now the scene in the ring changes as the matador begins what Andy calls his "passes." He keeps provoking the bull to charge his cape, then, at the very last minute, steps aside as the confused animal runs by. "*Olé*," everyone yells, just like in the movies. At first, Sheri is thrilled, but nervous too, looking between the action and that wife and child, worrying that something bad could happen. The child would see, be scarred for life. It's just a baby. It can't run, or even crawl.

"Looky looky," Andy says shaking his head as the famous matador begins a riskier set of moves, slipping in closer to the bull's horns, actually tapping its hip as it goes by him, then smirking. Sheri starts to feel sick watching him. Or it's the wine. She and Andy have finished their first bottle.

The bull comes around for another charge. The entire crowd

leans forward. But now Sheri's phone vibrates on her belt.

"Why'd ya let her do that?" says Andy, when she starts to get up.

Sheri hesitates. The question is valid—and unanswerable. She goes down the concrete steps and into the shadows of the bullring.

"It's coming, Sher," says Janet. "I asked for a Section."

"What? Now?"

"Yes, yes. I'm about to get the drip. Thank god." Her mother hates pain. "Roger's going to send you a picture as soon as they take it out."

"That's not necessary."

"You'll eat those words when you see your brother. Keep your phone on."

Returning to her seat, Sheri gets a look from Andy. She smiles weakly. How can she explain that you never get away from someone like Janet? That even here, she can't seem to rid herself of a growing sense of obligation towards that baby. Her brother.

Now the matador, whose hair has been thoroughly mussed from his efforts, walks to the side, pauses, and returns towards the wounded bull with a sword and a lofty expression. The audience murmurs. "It's time," says Andy, ominously.

"*Mátalo! Mátalo!*" Someone yells behind them. Sheri turns and sees that it's the woman with the fancy hair bun. She locks eyes with Sheri, her eyeliner giving her gaze a certain power, and nods for her to chime in: "*Mátalo!*" But Sheri can't locate her own blood thirst. She turns back to the ring, where the matador is slowly moving in, tiptoeing forward in his ballet flats and pink socks, gold tassels swinging over the edge of both shoulders, his sword pitched at a strange angle. It occurs to Sheri that her mother is on par with all of the world's great tormentors. Bullies. Bullfighters. Beautiful women. She is as vicious, as ridiculous.

"Oh my," says Andy, and he rises in his seat slightly, for now, in the ring, the matador meets the bull and strikes the sword between its shoulder blades right up to the hilt in a single, confident gesture. Sheri glances over and sees that the wife has turned her child around to watch. The baby, far from scarred by the sight, is waving its hands like an expert fan.

"Perfect kill," says Andy, and Sheri is almost hurt by this statement. Andy has a desire to accept things as they are, she sees now. The opposite of Janet. Except he's wrong: the bull, which should be dead, isn't. The matador's team runs it in tighter circles to make it fall, but the animal just turns on its feet like a dial and keeps going, blood pouring from its mouth in huge spurts that land on the brown-orange sand and on the matador's thighs.

Across the way, that baby is still cheering, but its mother has lost her smile.

Sheri returns her gaze to the bull, which is wavering, its rotation slowing. But it remains undeniably, inexplicably upright. She thinks of herself crawling over the rocks at the beach. The drunkenness she's been fuelling all afternoon suddenly fizzles and she has an almost overpowering impulse to rush down into the ring to touch this animal, feel its fur, get it out of there.

Now her phone vibrates. Again.

"Don' answer it," says Andy, without turning. "Don'."

The matador's team withdraws slightly, in awe of the sacrificial animal. The crowd is rapt. In their section, only Sheri's buzzing cell breaks the silence. The bull just stands there, alive, until the matador, less gracefully this time, tired, his bright socks sagging, his stiff jacket askew, his eyes wide with rage, yanks the sword back out of the animal's body, releasing a flood of blood.

The bull leans onto its forelegs, then simply tips into death. The matador walks away and begins a victory lap with his chin up, though the crowd is less than effusive. It has not been a perfect kill. The wife has recovered her look of loving support, but when she tosses her child's bootie towards her husband, it comes off as condescending. Other spectators are kinder, pitching flowers, a sheepskin of wine.

When he passes in front of the cheap seats, pasting on one of his handsome smiles to encourage applause, something lands at the matador's feet. He looks down, expecting another token, but instead finds something unusual disturbing the dust. A cell phone, vibrating. When he checks to see who's thrown it, Sheri refuses eye contact. She grabs Andy by the arm and pulls him, stumbling on his long legs, giggling, across several confused spectators, towards the exit.

MAKEOVER

I spotted myself at a Japanese hotdog stand. Me. Exactly as I am. No toppings on the dog, as I prefer, eating greedily, as I do. She shoved in the last bite with such recognizable eagerness that I can't say if it was disbelief or familiarity that stopped me cold. A taxi nearly ran me down before I stumbled across the street towards her—towards me.

"How?" I tried to say, but I couldn't speak. I stepped up onto the sidewalk and clutched the stand's cool metal edge. One of the young people staffing it bent down, his round, red hat on a tilt. "Hotdog?" he said, cheerfully.

This other person who was me—I'll call her "the other me"— was still only half visible. It was lunchtime and a popular spot. I could see her face, framed by short dark hair, like mine until recently (I had added highlights and was growing it out). She wore no makeup, as I normally did not. The skin around her eyes showed the precise signs of age that I had seen in my own features just minutes before, standing in a department store mirror down the block, asking myself if I needed to start using cosmetics. I had decided that I did and had allowed a salesperson to apply a faceful of them. I could still smell the powder she'd applied to my cheekbones while looking at me like a half decorated cake.

Then several people shifted out of the way and I saw the rest of her. My double. Sameness in the torso, the stance. Sameness in her wariness, which I could feel even at that distance. But there was one important difference: this woman's free hand was holding a stroller handle, pushing it gently back and forth. I stepped closer, incredulous, looking between the other me and her buggy.

She saw me. Our eyes met. Hazel on hazel. I thought I would freeze again, but now my shock was mobile. I circled slowly, as if before a mirror. I became momentarily lost in worry about my mental health. I saw myself in the straitjacket and padded room of movies. I saw my elderly father visiting me, wiping away my drool, trimming my toenails. He would resent every minute.

Someone gasped. I turned and could see people around the hotdog stand staring. Several more who were seated on a low brick fence nearby had stopped eating entirely, hotdogs horizontal, midair. The movie-like images in my mind switched to a montage of zombie horror. This crowd would become a mob. The young vendor would throw down his hat as he righteously dove forward with his long BBQ fork to pierce the hearts of each of us... aberrations.

I cleared my throat and forced myself to speak loudly enough to be overheard. "I. . . didn't expect to see you here. Shall we get lunch?... Like we enjoy doing? As *twins*."

The other me was still pushing her stroller back and forth in an automatic fashion. Her face was blank—her own version of shock, probably. She looked around, taking in people's unease. "Okay," she said, and immediately began pushing the stroller away.

I caught up to her. Neither of us looked back. At the next intersection, we hit a red light. "We have to get somewhere no one can see us," I said, thinking out loud. "I'll get the next cab— no, wait: the stroller. It won't fit. My place, then. It's close." As soon as I said it, I knew I didn't want that. My apartment was a sanctuary for one. How could I bring this other, a total stranger, there? "Actually... the concierge won't buy the twins thing. Forget that."

The other me said nothing, so I turned. There she was, grey, knees buckling. I reached over and grabbed her around the back, holding her up just in time. She was thinner than I'd thought myself to be, bony ribbed. Someone on her other side noticed her fainting too and took her arm. It was a young man in low-slung jeans and a hat that said "I'm HARD...to resist." "She okay?" he said, his voice not quite broken.

"We're fine," I said. "Low blood sugar."

"You should sit," he said, and pointed across the intersection to a chain bookstore that also housed a café.

Not knowing how to object to this reasonable suggestion, I steered the other me and stroller across the street, turning back once to see that the young man was still watching. I hoped he was exactly as he looked: someone who wouldn't care about us in two minutes. I waved and smiled eagerly, opened the café door, letting the other me in first, then lined up the stroller's wheels to wedge it inside.

The other me let herself fall into the nearest seat. I brought the stroller over and tried to get it out of people's way. It was so big and awkward. I had no experience with strollers.

"Thanks."

"Sure," I said, and went over to a side table where there was a pitcher of ice water and glasses. I poured a cup. The clinking ice made such a normal, healthily physical sound that I wanted it to go on forever.

The other me drank her water in three big gulps, the pink coming back into her cheeks. It was like watching someone colour in a black-and-white portrait of me.

She assessed me for the first time, which made me feel self-conscious, especially about my made-up face. I could almost hear my father, how, whenever I'd tried on lipstick or eyeshadow in high school, he had smirked, deadpanned, "Hollywood superstar." I don't even think he thought I looked bad. He didn't like the ambition of it.

The other me opened her mouth to talk, but a sharp wail emerged from the stroller. The baby. She stood and lifted it out from a heap of blankets. "Feeding time."

I nodded. She lifted her shirt and quickly put the infant to her breast—my breast! Except with huge, distorted nipples, based on what I saw before the baby seized one.

"Coffee?" I asked, disturbed, and also seeing that she was stuck there until it finished. She agreed to tea. I ordered and we sat in silence, steam from our cups mingling between us. Words kept rising and falling away before they made enough sense to utter, like water not quite reaching the boil. Twice, someone approached our table. "Uncanny!" said the first, an excitable woman we willed away. The other, a man with a smug mouth, said, "My daughter has triplets," as if this trumped every possible experience of likeness. But these intrusions subdued my panic. Everyone assumed we were twins now that we were sitting quietly together. We didn't have to fake it.

The other me rubbed her forehead. "What the fuck is happening?"

"I don't know."

"Who are you?"

"Who are you?" I replied, a bit defensively, because the other me's tone had been sharp, like an accusation, like she was the original, me the copy. I saw things differently. "And who is that?" I nodded towards the baby.

"She's mine."

"Well, I don't have a child."

"Why not?"

I didn't feel like answering this question. It was no one's business but my own. "That's personal."

The other me laughed for the first time. A rebuking laugh. "More personal than what's happening right now?"

I shook my head. I didn't enjoy explaining my choices to people. Why I was single. Why men had not been a consistent theme in my life. How each one I'd been close to had been tremendous, but the way an iceberg is, looming and fearsome too. I blamed this on my father, but no one needed to know so. The other me was different, obviously. She wanted to share. Yet we were the same, weren't we? I began to perspire from sheer confusion. I needed an explanation. Something sane-sounding, like ice on ice. "Facebook!" I said, my eyes widening. "I've seen memes where they put shots together. People who look the same—doppelgangers!"

The other me showed no optimism at this suggestion. In fact, she deflated, her eyelids drooping, as if my desperation made her feel resigned to some other truth. She lifted her free arm and shook it so that the long sleeve of her top fell towards the elbow, then lay her bare forearm on the table. Halfway up was an oblong birthmark. My hands began to tremble as, instinctively, I reached out to touch my own mark. She let her sleeve fall again with just a little too much satisfaction for my liking. "Okay," I said, still thinking on my feet. "So *could* you be my twin?"

It was her turn to shake her head. "I've seen pictures. I came alone."

"They could've faked them."

Annoyance disrupted her composure like tiny, local explosions she had to smooth over. Her eyes blinked fast. She licked her lips. "They didn't."

I realized that this is what I had done on countless occasions when I'd thought I could hide an inner battle against too much feeling, how anyone who had looked would've seen the effort. I shuddered at this insight; I'd never before understood how much people could know just by watching you sit and think.

"What's with the makeup?" she said.

"What about it?"

"It doesn't suit . . . you. Me. Whatever."

"Um, sorry, but do you get to say that?"

"This is all a big dream. I'll say what I want."

"It's not a dream."

"Even if it isn't. I don't like the makeup."

I tried to let the comment go. I had practice with letting things slide. Besides, part of me was bracing for a jolt. Something funny to break the tension. This would turn out like those TV bank ads—she had invested for retirement, I hadn't. Or gore was around the corner—this evil double had arrived to harvest my organs. I would be eviscerated, the café patrons traumatized. My boss would be without a sales team leader he could send anywhere, anytime, my father without anyone to systematical-ly undermine. In stories, meeting oneself is supposed to be like that. Something important. Corrective or horrific. But nothing was happening. I had met myself. She had a baby. I wore a mask of cosmetics. She seemed short-fused. She had questions. So did I. "What's it like?" I asked, nodding towards the baby.

The other me paused, then unplugged it from her breast and lifted it in my direction.

My eyes went wide. "I don't really know how…."

"It's not hard," the other me said, stiffly, transferring its weight into my hands, then ran a free hand over her hair.

"Aaah," I said, experiencing the heft of a real live baby. A girl, she said. I couldn't tell by the face, which looked like every other baby face.

"It's work," said the other me, answering my question from before. "But I don't mind."

I tilted the baby into a cradle position. What could she make of *my* face, I wondered. Her own mother's face, but with painted lips and coloured hair. She seemed to like it. I thought I saw her smile. Then a stream of yellowish breast milk emerged from one corner of her mouth.

"I see a person forming in there, now," the other me went on.

"I don't," I said, the warm milk soaking my sleeve. I stood and put her back into the stroller.

"You don't know her."

"Are you mad about this?" I asked, sitting back down.

"Why should I be mad?"

"You're judgmental."

"*You* sounded judgmental just now. Like I'm an idiot for having a baby. I could be free like you, right? Wandering the streets done up and wearing clothes designed for someone ten years younger."

"Okay. That's—you don't look so great yourself, you know." It was true. She was not only aging, as I was, she was obviously bone-tired. Her entire face sagged with fatigue.

"Fuck you," she said.

"You're just scared. Reacting to the weirdness."

"Nothing is as weird as giving birth," she said. "This is just—strange. You might not know the difference."

"You make it sound like this is my fault. I didn't ask to come across you. Or her."

"I think if these people really think we're twins, then they must be wondering why I look like a grownup and you look like an overgrown teenager."

"Stop it," I said, my voice rising. "Just stop." I swung my hand out in an accompanying gesture, accidentally pushing over her coffee mug, which landed in her lap.

The other me glared, then did something amazing. She pushed my own mug of coffee onto my lap. It lay in a lukewarm puddle on my skirt. Nearby, I heard someone clear her throat. People were looking.

I picked up the mug and brought a napkin to my thigh, but the other me got out of her chair and came over to my side. She pushed my shoulder aggressively. "You did it on purpose."

"What are you talking about? You just spilled *mine* on purpose."

She pushed my shoulder again, harder. I noticed her clothes for the first time. She wore ugly jeans with a too-high waist. Mom jeans without irony. Into them was tucked her faded, shapeless, long-sleeved cotton top. I stood. I had never been in a physical fight, except once, in Grade 7, when the class bully had made me fight someone else whom she'd chosen. She always enjoyed creating difficult situations for her minions. But all I could muster was a pinch to the girl's arm. Then I ran home crying and told my father, who was busy with a novel and with the final steps of rolling a cigarette, his lower lip slightly wet. He ran the paper over it and said, "We need bread." Now, I did not relish the idea of hitting my double. But I also found her negative reaction to me painful and unfair. I grabbed her arm as I had done in Grade 7 and squeezed it hard. Then I threw it back so that she spun around slightly. She struggled to regain her balance before lunging at me. In the next moment several people were surrounding us. A young woman from behind the counter stomped forward, opening and closing her arms like a ref telling someone they're out of a boxing match. "I'm calling security!"

The other me managed to scratch my face hard before someone with long, muscular fingers grabbed both my elbows and yanked me backwards. "Take 'er down a notch," said a man's voice in an accent I couldn't place. Rural.

The other me came forward again looking like she was going to hit me with a closed fist. I prepared for pain, or to awaken from the dream I knew this wasn't. But her baby started crying again, this time in a different pitch—hysterically, I thought. It screamed so hard that the café worker and the man with the muscled fingers both took a step back. *The twins have upset the child* was what they must've thought. They couldn't have accepted the reality that there were two of the same person present, that we had different lives, that we rejected one another's choices, that the baby was confused. If they had known, they might have ripped her from the stroller, warded us off with a crucifix, never let us touch her again.

The other me began organizing her things. She gritted her teeth and practically spat, "It's fine. We're fine. We fight, my twin and I. She'll sleep if I move—the baby, I mean."

"She thinks I'm prettier than you," I said, my blood boiling. I bent past the other me, who seemed tense in the extreme, on the verge of strangulation. But now we had the attention of the entire café, and she held herself in check. I brought my face to within inches of the baby's. "It's true, isn't it?" I asked her. Her crying stopped and her bumpy, potato-like features smoothed as they had in my arms. In her formlessness, her thoughts were completely invisible, but I told myself that she knew: I was the one, the original. Like a psychic who once called to me as I passed her kiosk on my way into a conference centre in Vegas, who said: "I see you for what you are."

I kissed the child. Her face crinkled up again and she screamed.

"She's overtired," the other me said with finality. "We'll go."

"Okay." I said, standing. What else could I do?

People started to relax. The café worker had not called security. The man whose strong fingers had saved us returned to a table where he whispered something to a woman who seemed proud of him for intervening.

I turned to the other me. Another mirror experience: age, the marks of a life half lived; two hysterics, two chumps, doubled, but half as self-assured as before. I felt compelled, suddenly, illogically, to hug her and took her in my arms. She did not return the gesture. She was holding back, almost like she was waiting for the jolt I'd expected earlier, something extreme that would justify fuller release. That she didn't recognize this as that moment angered me, and I also gave less than I might have.

As our awkward embrace ended, I reflected on the fate of the baby, what she could expect from knowing and being known, from having a parent, eventually leaving her childhood behind for adulthood, and then, in time, aging too. My face must've fallen, because the other me smiled without malice for the first time, and I caught the expression I'd seen in photos of myself, when I'd assessed my smile as inoffensive, but which had photographed as impatient, contrived. I smiled too, trying to convey acceptance—of her departure, my inevitable separation from the child. Yet I was no longer sure how to judge what I was putting into the world through my face or body. Then, thinking I might use the restroom to deal with the scratch on my face. I said my goodbyes.

When the café door closed on the other me though, I didn't feel like moving. Generic music was playing. I lingered, listening, people watching me. It might've been delayed shock, but I was relieved to be rid of her, of both of them.

The very first man who'd approached us, with the smug mouth and triplet granddaughters, returned. "Don't get much alone time, eh?" he said, looking me over.

Oddly, it was these words that most upset me that afternoon. The veneer of everydayness seeped from the moment like make-up remover smearing mascara. Starkly, I could feel where I was in space, who I was in time. Unable to reply, I looked at him blankly, then rushed to the restroom where, ignoring the throbbing scratch, I touched up my face.

RUN

Erin Martin lives in a condo near the lakeshore. Her place is pale and spare, carefully composed like a still life. Besides Erin, who spends little time there, the only things that seem to move through the apartment are the clean smells of her things. When she opens her front hall closet, a whiff of light perfume comes off her jackets. Over her puffy duvet, in the bedroom that is walled on two sides by large windows, floats the scent of fresh laundry detergent mixed with cotton. Often Erin buys a single calla lily and stands it among pebbles in a heavy, square glass vase that she leaves in the centre of her small supper table so that the eating area is also pleasantly fragrant.

Every morning Erin runs on the treadmill at the gym inside her building. Then she showers and takes the streetcar the short distance to work, stopping on the way to pick up a coffee, which serves as breakfast. Erin is a junior equity analyst for a brokerage house, and though business has suffered due to the recent market crisis, her job appears to be secure. In part this is because Erin is so upbeat, prompt and detail-oriented. But she also reveres financial modelling, to which she ascribes a near-magic potential to foretell the future (the crisis was an exception, the result of a few corrupt individuals colluding to make this impossible). Erin exudes a sense of pride at being part of the process of wealth creation. She finds it funny that some people would characterize this enthusiasm as greed. She has never seen it that way. Prosperity is what everyone strives for. All one hundred percent of them.

She often has lunch at one of the good places on King Street. Usually she orders salad. Most nights, after work, which ends late, she goes for drinks and dinner with people from her office. While she's had more than one long relationship, she has been unattached for some time. Occasionally, she lets herself be taken home by some man after these evenings, but never anyone from her office, and never to her apartment. She prefers to keep her home free of good or bad memories of that kind.

On Saturday Erin goes out with a running group. Together, they are training for a marathon. She has bought a new wicking shirt from the store where the group meets, which keeps her dry and cool over long distances. As Erin runs, she finds that her mind is blank, and often she can't remember which route they have followed. She comes back to herself only when she has stopped and gone home to take a long, unhurried shower in her bathroom, knowing she has the rest of the day to do as she pleases. This time is usually spent shopping with a girlfriend, seeing a film or reading magazines. Erin has a large circle of acquaintances but doesn't consider anyone her best friend. She finds many women needy. She also hates malls and prefers the shops on Queen West or in Yorkville. Yorkville is where she gets her hair cut every few weeks, at a salon-spa. Erin enjoys her spa time and justifies the extra expense by reminding herself that she hasn't found any other comparable relief to the stress of her job. She lets her newly-painted toes curl over the cool pebbles that form the spa's floor and thinks of how everyone who works there is so kind, about how remarkably well-groomed they are. Erin can't stand people who are not put together. They seem to her to have lost control of something crucial. When she was in university, the popular look was sloppy and slutty. Everyone wore low-rise jeans or pink sweat pants with words like "Sweet" on the rear. Erin avoided most of that period's influence and laughs when she looks through pictures from her all-girls' residence and sees again her floormates dressed like off-duty strippers. When Erin laughs, her small nose crinkles and her grey eyes narrow. Little can be judged by looking into those eyes, but people often try. Erin works at looking like someone you would want to know, and for the most part she succeeds.

Her family lives in a nearby city. They approve of her path in life and never nag her about getting married. Erin visits them for all the important holidays and speaks to her mother, a legal secretary, once a week over the phone. Erin's younger brother lives in Korea, where he teaches English, a circumstance Erin cannot fathom. She has visited him there, but would not venture outside of Seoul to the remote provincial capital where he lives, apparently happily. Their visit was warm but brief, Erin having gone on to a yoga retreat in Bali. Due to distance, then, she and her brother have grown apart. Erin loves her family and keeps a picture on her fridge of them standing together by Georgian Bay, but she sees herself as a woman on her own and she likes it that way. Some nights she falls asleep by imagining that the story of her life will resemble that of movie characters she admires. She knows love will eventually find her, when the time is right, and, in the meantime, she should live well and for herself.

After work one rainy spring night, Erin is out with two journalists from a business news service. She is bored. Her boss, the senior analyst, had put this meeting off forever, and has finally requested that she go in his place. They meet at a bar Erin immediately dislikes. Near Chinatown, it has zero style. Journalists are always cheap. They're also suspicious and devious, always angling for inside information. The work she has to do to impress these two men will bring her little reward, she knows. Meanwhile, she has to tolerate them as they gently prod her for tidbits about the companies she follows. Worse, she finds both men unattractive. One looks to be about forty, overweight. The other could be her own age, but he's already bald. He wears a terrible green suit and talks incessantly about his new car. Erin orders clams in white wine sauce but has very little appetite. The men eat heartily and drink beer throughout dinner. They begin to annoy her by retreating into themselves, talking about the one man's renovation to his garage, the other's plan to apply for a foreign posting.

Erin excuses herself to use the bathroom. On the way, she notices a woman from her running group sitting at a full table. She overhears the woman laughing and commenting to her companions about the TV show *The Bachelor*, where women compete to become engaged to one eligible man. In the bathroom, Erin thinks about the woman, whose name, she recalls, is Patricia. She looked like she was in total control of the conversation. Her head was thrown back as she laughed at her own joke. She had a hand pressed lightly to her neck, emphasizing its length and her abandon.

On the way back from the bathroom, Erin decides to stop and say hello. As she gets up close, it's apparent that everyone in the group is quite drunk. Patricia, who is still talking, stops when she sees Erin and gives her a long look, from head to toe. It takes Patricia a moment to find her smile again.

Erin blushes. "I was just passing…"

"Erin, right?"

"Yes. From running group. And you're Patricia."

"Everyone, this is Erin from my running group."

Everyone nods. Erin is aware that her sobriety is making her uninteresting to them, an interruption to their good time.

"Join us for a drink, Erin!" someone says, finding an obvious solution to everyone's discomfort.

"Yes… Erin, good idea!" says Patricia emphatically. "In fact, maybe you can help us out. We're wondering how they keep finding people to try out for *The Bachelor*. Forty women who all look like—well, like you, Erin. They all look like you and they are killing themselves to get engaged to this one guy! Where do they make people like you?"

Everyone at the table is looking at Erin. There are six of them, including one other woman, serious-looking and beautiful. Patricia, whom Erin finds too sharp-featured to be pretty, is nonetheless attractively thin, with nearly emerald eyes. The four men are indistinguishably ordinary and casually dressed. They look excited. As though they are visiting from out of town. Erin can't tell by looking at them what they do for a living. She remembers that Patricia works for some charity. Patricia's words, "like you, Erin," stick in Erin's ear. They were used insultingly, she thinks, and also as a challenge. Erin feels that if she leaves the table, she will look foolish.

"Sure, just a quick drink," she says, ignoring the last question.

"Fabulous," says Patricia, raising a stick arm towards a waiter, who quickly delivers a fresh pitcher of beer and a glass and chair for Erin. Apparently, beer is what this bar specializes in. No one at the table seems to mind.

"Now, Erin, what is it that you do again?"

"I'm an equity analyst."

"Analysis. Yes. Right. Are you involved, Erin?"

"Patricia," says the other woman at the table, who appears more sober than the rest and maybe more aware of Patricia's games.

"It's okay, no worries," says Erin. "No, I'm not seeing anyone right now."

"Not for lack of offers, I'm sure," says one of the men, two seats away from Erin. He smiles widely. He looks like a thousand men Erin has met before. She returns the smile neutrally.

"I'm sure not!" says Patricia. "But seriously, would you do what those girls are doing on the show? Would you compete for the right guy? I mean, what really makes women like you tick, Erin?"

"Patricia," the woman at the table says again. "We've been here since three," she says to Erin, by way of explanation.

Erin looks at Patricia, who leans over the table like she's about to reveal a secret. Her dark, straight hair, which is cut in an expensive-looking shag, swings forward and catches the light. Her eyes seem to do two things at once. They shine, and, Erin thinks, they do some math.

"Personally," Patricia says, "I see no problem with the whole harem set-up as long as the women are smart enough to get what they need from each other when Mr. Big Shot's off with one of his chosen ones. What do you say?" Not waiting for an answer, she tips back laughing. Her hand finds her throat as it did earlier, as if to feel for the laughter in there. The men all snicker, maybe considering the possibilities. Erin notices Patricia's long nails and finds herself wondering if Patricia has ever been to her spa. She imagines Patricia sitting in the sauna with her legs crossed, dropping one of the thick white robes they give clients, then sitting naked and laughing.

There's a pause. Patricia looks around the table speculative-ly. Everyone seems tense. She reaches over to one of the men and pulls him by the chin over to her, giving him a long, open-mouthed kiss. Erin blushes again. The beautiful woman smiles tightly. Patricia puts her other hand behind the man's ear. When she pulls away, she lifts her hand and, opening it, produces a gold coin. "See, Erin? You have to get what you need. Just what you need." Everyone laughs, and the man in question applauds the trick with an overly enthusiastic clap.

"Slow down there," she says, giving him a disdainful look. "Getting what you need, one must also be careful." And reaching behind another of the men's heads, she appears to pull from his hairline a wrapped, fluorescent orange condom. Everyone but Erin laughs and hoots.

"Erin?"

The younger journalist in the green suit, who must have finally noticed Erin's absence, has come over. Erin nearly jumps from her seat with relief. As she leaves the table, she is conscious of the unfamiliar smell of beer on her breath. Patricia is still training a snarky smile on her when she turns to say, with a friendly smile she realizes is misplaced, "See you at running."

But in the weeks that follow this encounter the weather in the city remains unseasonably wet. Almost no one shows up for running group, including Patricia. Erin keeps pace with the rest in her DryCELL warm-up jacket, but feels that her state of mind is less peaceful than usual. She notices that one of the parks the group regularly passes through is unnecessarily and annoyingly strewn with litter. Two weeks in a row she wears a fanny pack and carries out some trash.

She visits *The Bachelor* website and watches the first episode of the most recent season. She disagrees that the women on the show look like her. Most of them wear too much makeup, too much pink. They overdo their hair. But she won't deny some resemblance. She wonders what this means, if anything. Generally, she sees nothing wrong with the concept of the program, which is quite entertaining, and thinks the women look good overall. By her third episode Erin begins to favour one contestant, named

Donna, a twenty-eight-year-old who is less scheming than some of the other women, more natural looking.

At the office one day, Erin notices herself laughing a fake laugh for her boss's sake—something she has done without a grudge countless times in the past. Part of the job. But this time she wonders how she looks while she laughs, how someone like Patricia might judge her if the moment were taped and played back.

One evening, Erin is leaving a bar uptown. It's pouring rain again, and she's about to lift her arm in her shiny raincoat to hail a cab when she notices a woman on the other side of the street. Erin freezes, realizing the woman is Patricia. She is not wearing a coat. The next moment, a second woman comes up behind Patricia and takes her by the arm, swinging her around roughly. Patricia resists and makes an almost comical attempt to pull away. The woman is tall and strong-looking. She doesn't let go and maintains what looks like a painful hold on Patricia's arm. It's late and a weeknight and there aren't many people around. A cab pulls up in front of Erin. "Where to?" asks the driver through the open passenger-side window. Across the street, the woman is shaking Patricia, who is saying, loudly enough to be heard at a distance, even in the rain, "No more, Nancy. I'm getting out. I'm out!" Her shiny hair is stuck to her head as though she's been pulled from a pool, and her dress is soaked. She appears to be missing a heel on one shoe.

The cab driver says something to Erin and revs his motor impatiently. Erin looks across the street once more. Everything in her wants to get in the cab and go. But she keeps looking across the street where she sees the tall woman do something startling. She slaps Patricia across the face, hard. Then the woman starts dragging Patricia back in the direction they've come from, still holding her arm like an irate mother.

"Patricia!" Erin calls out.

Both women turn. Patricia makes eye contact. Her face changes. She looks fearful. She shakes her head, like "no." The other woman also looks Erin's way—it's the same beautiful woman from the bar. She immediately lets go of Patricia's dress and smoothes the material of her trench coat before smiling at Erin and walking quickly away in the opposite direction.

Patricia hurries across the street, limping on her single heel, and opens the door to the cab. Erin does the same on the other side. Inside, Patricia drips all over the back seat. Erin isn't sure what to say.

"Where you headed?" snaps the cabbie, openly angry now to be wasting his time.

"Wherever you live," says Patricia, looking up at Erin. "Let's go there."

Erin almost says no. But Patricia is shaking with cold. Erin gives the driver her address and he pulls away. Patricia looks back out the rear window more than once, as if trying to see whether the other woman is following them. Otherwise, she is silent.

Erin smiles at the concierge on the way through the lobby of her building, but he doesn't return it. He is not accustomed to seeing her return with anyone, let alone a hobbling, strikingly thin, soaking-wet woman. Erin ignores his concerned scowl and presses the elevator button.

In her apartment she offers Patricia a towel to dry her hair, but she refuses. "Can I take a shower?"

"It's down there," says Erin, and shows her to the bathroom.

While the shower runs, Erin stands beside one of her living-room windows, staring down into the wet, reflective city. She tries to work out what must have gone on between Patricia and the tall, aggressive woman, wonders if she's right to think they are lovers, or have been. She remembers that one Saturday, at her running group, she saw Patricia kneeling in front of one of the men, rubbing his calf, kneading it with her thin hands. There was something sensual about the way she did it. Erin wonders now if this had been an overture, or maybe nothing, whether Patricia likes both men and women.

Patricia startles her from these thoughts, emerging from the bathroom and approaching at a deliberately slow pace wrapped in one of Erin's smaller towels. Erin feels like she should look away. She recalls the image of this woman at the spa and wonders what is about to happen—here, in her home.

"Don't flatter yourself," Patricia says. "I'll be out of here in a minute. I just need something to wear."

Erin obliges, going into her room to pick out some clothes, but worries about giving them to a stranger. She and Patricia don't even know each other's last names. Will she ever get them back? Still, she can't make someone else wear her old painting clothes. She chooses decent pants and a top, beige mid-calf socks, black flats.

"Thanks," says Patricia, and goes back into the bathroom to change.

"Is everything okay?" Erin calls back to her. "With that other woman, I mean."

"No problem," Patricia replies. Now that she's clean and dry, Patricia's voice has started to sound strong again, the edge coming back into it. "It was just a stupid argument."

"But you looked—I don't know. Like you were in trouble."

"Hey," says Patricia, coming back into the room, shaking the last drips out of her straight hair with the towel. "It's no big deal. She and I have our own thing. Don't be jealous." She smiles and approaches Erin, puts a hand on her cheek. "You're sweet."

Erin sees that, dressed in the clothes she's been given, Patricia could pass for her older sister—something Erin always wished she'd had. She swallows hard, asks Patricia if she wants some tea. Patricia snorts. "You don't even try to turn it off in your own home, do you?"

"Turn what off?"

"Your whole tea and cookies with a side of cute routine."

"It's not a routine."

"Maybe not." Patricia looks uncertain for a moment. Like the thought that Erin is being herself frightens her. "I'm not one to talk about routines. Anyway. Can you call me a cab?"

Ten minutes later, Erin's cell rings: Patricia's taxi is downstairs. At the door Patricia asks her for cab fare. When Erin hands her forty dollars, Patricia touches her cheek again. "See you at running," she says, but the words are saturated with sarcasm. Then she steps into the hall and is gone.

The following week, the wholesome woman on *The Bachelor* impresses the man during a dancing date on a yacht, while two of her competitors are denied a prize rose—the ultimate rebuff, signalling that the bachelor had lost interest and they have to pack their bags and go home. At the very end of the episode, there's a video in which the wholesome woman speaks to the camera, saying she's sorry to see the other women, whom she calls her "new friends," leave. The interview is shot in a garden somewhere, a place teeming with flowers. The sun lights the woman's hair so that it glows. She tells the camera she is happy to have made it as far as she has. That she is lucky, really. And she is just hoping for the best, nothing more, nothing less. She wears a pale blue V-necked sweater, and her tiny beige shorts are pleated. Erin rewinds the scene several times, scrutinizing the woman and, on the third or fourth viewing, begins to question whether she has told the truth.

Erin arrives early at her running group the following Saturday and waits for Patricia. She hopes they can run together, maybe talk more about what happened that rainy night. Erin admits to herself that she finds Patricia sexy. Though she has never slept with a woman, and a storyline in which she ends up with one does not match any of the scenarios she has had in mind for her future, she is excited at the prospect of getting to know this edgy, mysterious woman. But the toll on attendance resulting from the recent bad weather has not lessened. Only three people besides their coach show up, and Erin starts her run lethargically. It's no longer raining, but as they go along the lake, a sharp wind whips her in the face, which makes her feel more miserable. Even the lake, which she normally loves to observe from above, through her apartment windows, seems drab today, its slate grey waves cold and uninviting. Just fifteen minutes in she is out of breath and has to stop. Erin is unused to feeling both unhappy and tired. She decides that she should ramp up her workout schedule. Her marathon is only six weeks off. It would be such a failure if she didn't finish. She hasn't been herself lately. Why does she care in the least about Patricia? She's no one. Probably in some kind of twisted relationship with that other woman.

Erin gets back into her run and, pushing herself, ignoring her own discomfort, finishes ahead of the others. Her coach gives her a congratulatory slap on the back and she feels proud. Then, behind her, Erin hears two men from the group talking about Patricia. Not wanting to be noticed eavesdropping, Erin bends down and undoes the laces of one of her sneakers. One of the men, a lawyer named Bill, says something in a low voice, which Erin strains to hear but can't.

"... didn't have her pegged as the type, myself, but you don't know. You just don't fucking know," replies the other man, Bill's running partner, whose name Erin can't remember.

"No, I guess you don't. She was in it with another woman."

"Oh, I could've told you that much. Pat and her took me for drinks once. Glad I didn't get too deep into it."

"Lucky you."

"Yeah, well, lucky them. Big money while it lasted. And then bang! Off the map."

"Someone'll go down. Lotsa guys went for it. Thinking with the wrong head."

The men laugh. Erin tries to stand but feels her knees weaken. One of the men touches her waist. It's Bill.

"You okay, Erin?"

"I just need to walk it out a bit."

"Just take it easy," he says, and gives her a little squeeze.

Later, at home, Erin sits for a long time staring down at her uneaten lunch. She takes the elevator downstairs and asks the concierge for the weekend newspaper. He tells her he's all out but that he can send his trainee out to the store. Erin flashes him her smile of gratitude, then catches herself and says more seriously, "I'd appreciate it." He keeps smiling back at her. She wonders what it would take to convince people that she is not someone worth knowing, worth going out of your way to please. Ten minutes later, the trainee knocks on her door and hands her the paper. In the City section she finds it. "Extortion Ring Targeted Brokerage Employees." The article explains how a man became an informant for police after he suspected that the woman he was having an affair with was going to blackmail him. Police used a wire to record several meetings with the woman, who went by the alias "Patricia." Police say someone must have tipped off the women because they have disappeared.

Putting down the paper abruptly, Erin walks to her bathroom. She tries to imagine Patricia in there, looking at herself in the mirror, using that small towel to dry herself, putting on Erin's own pants. Erin opens her drawer beside her sink where she keeps extra cosmetics. The basket, normally overflowing with lipsticks, eyeliners and nail polish in last year's shades, is half full.

On Monday she returns to work and is sitting at her desk after one of her sector's quarterly teleconferences. Outside, the city is brilliantly sunny. Everyone in the office is talking about the improvement in the weather and the hope that European markets will stabilize thanks to an influx of central bank cash. A friend calls and Erin speaks to her briefly. The friend wants to get together with some guys they know for drinks and dinner after work. Erin tells her she isn't feeling well. When 6:30 p.m. finally arrives and she is free to go, Erin passes her boss's office door without her usual waves and smiles. She decides to walk home.

She is wearing inappropriate shoes, but doesn't really care if she wrecks them. She has so many pairs. She thinks consciously about spring weather for the first time in years, and remembers a day when she was small when it rained so hard, falling in silver sheets, that she and her brother went down the front steps of their house barefoot in their shorts and T-shirts and pretended to swim across the lawn for what seemed like hours. The grass had turned nearly to muck under their feet as they zigzagged around, pushing out their mouths and flapping their hands open and closed beside their faces, making like fish. They slipped all over the lawn, comically falling and getting up, falling and getting up. Then the early May sun came out, ending their fantasy, and they shivered like leaves until their mother brought them each a towel and hurried them inside, where they laughed some more as they tried to peel away their muddy layers.

Erin has planned to watch the next episode of *The Bachelor*—the one that could decide the fate of the wholesome-looking girl. But as she crosses Front Street, in the shadow of one of the city's tallest towers, Erin knows that she doesn't care what happens and won't watch after all. She has a frightening moment in which she can't ascertain what caring is, exactly, what it means for anyone to care what happens to anyone else, what it would mean to her colleagues if she didn't show up for work one day, how she herself would feel if the rain from the past several weeks had swept her condominium into the Great Lake and sent her favourite glass vase to the bottom to sink forever into the muck.

She understands that Patricia is somewhere right now, smiling, likely wearing Erin's lipstick, her throat exposed. She got away. Has gone with the other woman—or others—to start a new racket in a new city. Buenos Aires. Berlin. Maybe she will join another running group there, where she can tell her unlikely story of working for a charity, and people like Erin will believe her because they don't really care what she says or what she really does at night when no one else is around to see, while in their own apartments they sleep, their running shoes lined up neatly in front closets, below jackets for every season and every sport, twenty stories up, slowly drying out.

BACKUP

She walked into the kitchen, where the manager was standing beside one of the dishwashers with a hand on his back, bending to look inside. Another man, who would normally have been stacking dishes into its racks, stood beside him with an untied apron hanging from his neck.

"I'm leaving," she said. She ran a finger along the back of her collar. Her blouse was black, button-down, conservative. Her knee-length skirt was tight, also black. Nametags weren't used in the restaurant, but if she'd had one, it would have read "Mel" instead of her full name, Mélanie, because that's how people at work knew her. Her hair was up, though sections drooped out. Her lipstick was nearly gone. It was very hot in the kitchen.

"Ha-ha," said the manager, who did not turn to look. He was watching the silent, broken-down dishwasher as if repairing it with his eyes. Out of deference, the other man did the same, exaggerating the intensity of his stare. The manager had a fake tan and a chest that had been worked into a wide V on a bench press. All around them the kitchen was in motion. Pans hissed and flames shot up. Three sous-chefs retrieved prepped ingredients from large, labeled containers, tonging things into place. A cook went into the freezer as another stepped towards a separate counter near the exit with two full plates. Putting them down, his hands nearly touched those of a waitress who had come in from the dining room to stand there expectantly. She wore the same kind of black-on-black blouse and skirt combination as Mélanie. She was smiling under her sweaty makeup, though. Mélanie didn't smile.

"Greg. Will you pay me out for my last week? I'm leaving."

"What am I, accounts? I'm not hearing this," he said, stiffening in his bent-over position. "Jesus. Get back out there."

"I don't work here anymore. But I won't go until you give me my pay."

The manager finally stood. "You're quitting. Now. While I'm short-staffed. And with this." He gestured at the cavernous dishwasher. "You are actually that much of a bitch."

"Just pay me and I'm gone."

That manager was like others before who had restrained a doubt when hiring Mélanie and had ended up regretting it. She was young, had the body they were after, and her face seemed composed. But these men—they were all men—saw something else too, something that didn't suit their agenda. They could never guess what it was, and always seemed frustrated by weighing an unknown risk against an otherwise good package. The risk always materialized. Mélanie was like a substitute teacher; anyone could see she was competent, smart even. She could perform cheeriness. But she never fit in with the other wait staff and didn't try to. She seemed to be doing her job on the other side of an invisible wall. In each case, over time, this became an irritation to managers. Customers picked up on the difference too. Maybe trying to pierce the barrier between them and the good-looking woman serving their food, they were often rude to her—more so, even, than wait staff are used to. Eventually, Mélanie dropped her cheerful demeanour and left, always abruptly, always with a degree of regret. Like other subs, she was not missed.

Two restaurants before the one with the broken dishwasher, during six months when Mélanie tried living in Kelowna, she'd let herself be befriended by a hostess at a steakhouse. They swapped stories about their respective hometowns, went for drinks even. One evening, finishing her pint, distracted by a hockey game on a nearby screen, Mélanie absently hummed the melody of the song that was playing over the sound system, then sang some of the lyrics. The hostess, whose reasons for wanting to be Mélanie's friend were never clear except that she seemed partial to outsiders, covered her mouth and pointed. She'd heard that voice before. "That's you!" she said, and clapped excitedly, struggling to recall the details. "You were in the video! Oh my god!" The song was by someone famous—who? The hostess couldn't recall the name. "How did you end up here?" she asked, her clapping trailing off. She was thirty—outright old by the standards of the restaurant world and eight years Mélanie's senior. She shouldn't even have been a hostess anymore, but no one had ever bothered to promote her to a service position. The hostess didn't seem to mind. She emanated a relaxed willingness to wait and see what more, if anything, life had in store for her. Mélanie liked this. It was the reason they had become, if not real friends, at least friendly. But hearing Mélanie's voice on the sound system had opened up something ambitious inside her, and for the rest of the evening she'd repeated, over and over, as she became quite drunk, "You have to go back to singing." For all her years and her experience, though, that woman didn't know anything about going back.

After high school and before waitressing, Mélanie had been a backup singer, one of three who'd toured with the female singer-songwriter whose song the hostess recognized, probably from having seen the video on the Canadian country music TV channel, where it ran, for a time, in moderate rotation. Before that, Mélanie grew up in a Northern town where a choir director had been the most important influence in her life. She had been his best student for a lot of years, and singing had been her whole existence. The choir director had made her his own, in secret, and so singing had become an aspect of fuller training for Mélanie, had been a way through to adulthood that included pleasure, but also deception, and the constant strain, like a repetitive tension track in a Hollywood movie, of the choir director's unwillingness for her to grow up, to leave, to explore her talents on her own.

On her eighteenth birthday, Mélanie mailed a demo to several management companies along with a video her younger brother shot of her dancing and singing. In it, she wore her only set of heels and a red tube dress she'd ordered online from the label Bebe. Six months after that, she got one call. A company wanted a meeting in Vancouver. The evening before it was to take place, she went into her parents' living room. They were watching the news. She said, "I'm going over to Britney's for the night." Both nodded without looking over. Then Mélanie walked to the bus station and got on the night bus. Arriving in downtown Vancouver early the next morning, she went to sit on a stone bench near a huge modern fountain across the street from the company's offices until it was time to go in. Her thrill at being there attached itself to the movement of the water, and she watched it like a movie.

Inside, a receptionist led her down a hallway. When the meeting room door opened, Mélanie saw two young men in extremely hip clothes coming towards her. "Mel!" they chimed, as if they were all friends. Behind them and to one side, sitting silently on a white couch, was the singer-songwriter, whom Mélanie recognized right away, but who was, in person, disconcertingly small and delicate, with squinty, cool eyes. She stayed seated. Eventually, she said she was pleased to "meet the girl attached to the voice." Everything about her conveyed impatient judgment, which reminded Mélanie so much of the choir director that she was glad when the woman excused herself. Mélanie and the company people talked for maybe ten minutes more. Her bus back north left four hours later.

It was only the following month, after they'd called again, this time to tell Mélanie they would be willing to try her out on a short contract, that she told her parents. They disapproved. So she asked her brother to pool the savings from his part-time job with her own so that she could afford to stay somewhere— anywhere—in Vancouver until she got paid, which he did readily. Together they searched Craigslist and found her a furnished room. Then she called the choir director and told him he would never see her again. His car screeched to a halt outside her house minutes later, but he didn't dare go up the walk. Mélanie's father had once threatened him with his hunting gun. Mélanie closed her bedroom curtains and packed with a knotted stomach. She had never pictured herself singing backup for someone else, but it was a sensible option. The company must have seen her potential to play a supporting role. Her voice was clear, strong and trained. Her demo video had shown them that she could dance. But Mélanie guessed that it had also captured something else: the mask she wore for others, which, she knew from having studied herself in the mirror while performing with a hairbrush microphone for many hours, over many years, looked like eagerness incarnate.

Mélanie met the other two backup singers on her first real day in Vancouver and was told to get to know them and to practice with them as a team until she had the songs down. One of the women, Kassandra, had long legs and a heart-shaped face. Mélanie expected her to be vivacious, but when Kassandra spoke, her words rolled out in a steady drone, and she avoided most eye contact. She was also Black—Mélanie's first Black acquaintance. Where Mélanie came from, people were a Heinz 57 of European backgrounds—Irish, Scottish, a few Ukrainians, and, less often, French-Canadian, like she was. Or they were Native. But most were White. That's what the other singer was: big like a basketball player, with enormous breasts, and really white. Yet she was supple too, almost like she was made of some other material than just skin and bones, something softer. Bethanne was her name, and she had been with the singer-songwriter for a year already. She came up with all the moves and showed Mélanie and Kassandra everything. One sequence she taught them was the kind girl groups like the Supremes used to do. The left arm, then the right, would come down in succession, the hands and fingers twittering slightly, snaking. While they did this, their hips would also move. Left together and downward. Then right together and back up. Even though she had natural rhythm, Mélanie found it hard to keep all of this straight. It was the opposite of choir, where she would get stern, reprimanding looks from the director if he noticed her hands or feet beating out time.

In Mélanie's first stage shows, she depended on both women. Kassandra had a deliberate way of moving and a deep, husky singing voice that rarely faltered. Much like offstage, she kept her gaze fixed off in the distance. In shows, this conveyed the impression that the music was transporting her far away, and audiences loved her. Mélanie trusted her and leaned heavily on those experienced vocals. But Kassandra didn't lead. It was Bethanne's profile and her shoulders, nearly touching those of the other two women, who stood on either side of her, that kept the backup line functioning. Mélanie learned to work her voice in better and better harmony as part of this threesome, either behind the mic stand or using her headset, depending on the song, and her faith came to rest more and more on Bethanne's shoulders. If Bethanne had ever stopped or lost her rhythm, Mélanie felt like she would have fallen down or walked offstage. Knowing this, fear bit at her. She often pictured the choir director sitting behind the glaring stage lights, watching for missteps. Only Bethanne's big, safe body could override the image.

Meanwhile, Mélanie and Bethanne became friends. On the tour bus they sat together watching power lines slung between poles along farmers' fields, then city buildings come up around them or fall away. They synched seat-back screens on airplanes to share movies. At hotels they got together in the late afternoon, after rehearsals, to talk or to play card games, of which Bethanne knew many. They played Rummy 500, or crib using Bethanne's travel-sized board. On days when Kassandra joined them, they switched to euchre, her favourite.

Though Mélanie had never gone anywhere before she moved to Vancouver, she thrived in this life of travel. Its rigour and repetition reminded her of musical training. Wherever they went, a sameness prevailed that comforted her. In emails to her brother, she usually described the sights she'd taken in: Pike Place Market, Banff, the Golden Gate Bridge. But visiting these places made Melanie feel next to nothing. What she enjoyed, though found impossible to describe in her emails, were the transfers between places, the requirement of alarm clocks, transportation, a strict rehearsal schedule, and the exhausting shows. Every night Mélanie took her time removing her stage makeup, safe in the knowledge that she would next apply it, sing, bow, exit and take it off elsewhere, in the same order. The comfort she took from repetition was not public. In the company of nearly everyone on the tour, especially the singer-songwriter, she wore her mask, pretending to be that amazed, innocent child of a mill town whom her brother had captured on film for her demo. But she wasn't. She was born to tour. Only Bethanne knew so. But on this point, they starkly diverged.

Bethanne had a real home and a husband. Mélanie met him during a month-long touring break during which the singer-songwriter went to Salt Spring to write more songs. Mélanie asked the management company for an interim gig, but they said it wasn't possible. She counted the days until the tour bus would leave again. When Bethanne invited her and Kassandra over to her house in Vancouver's East End, she accepted.

The house was unremarkable from the outside, and cramped and dingy inside, without enough lighting to save most corners from shadow, or any discernible logic to the furnishings. A cracked mirror leaned against the wall of the main hallway; one chair sat upside down on another, scratched legs in the air. None of the women made much money singing backup—much less than most people imagined. They kept quiet about it. The singer-songwriter had made it clear plenty of girls would be happy to take their places. But the dinginess Mélanie found at Bethanne's didn't result only from lack of money. Mélanie had noticed a similar dishevelment in Bethanne herself, an untidiness she disliked but which she had accepted as part of Bethanne's generally loose, unfussy way. Seeing the house made Mélanie wonder whether, in time, this acceptance would waver.

He wasn't perfect. He was as compact as Bethanne was big. He'd obviously had his nose broken at some point, certainly before his marriage to Bethanne, which had happened not two years before. He looked sombre, as though something had upset him and he was puzzling it out, searching for resolution but not finding it. When he and Mélanie were introduced, though, he seemed to let go of this trouble entirely, like someone who has been startled drops a ball. Then he let a smile turn his small mouth into something inviting. A sliver of apple. He extended his hand. It was the hand of a piano player, Mélanie believed, and taking it, she experienced a surge, like her blood was suddenly too hot.

As it turned out, he had nothing to do with music. He was an animator who worked contracts, though Mélanie gathered there were never enough of these. He seemed disillusioned, maybe had expected Bethanne's career to take off with more speed and incline to make up for his own slow fizzle. Unlike Bethanne, whose aura filled whatever room she stepped into, Luke's seemed to project no further than the very spot he was occupying, a difference Mélanie ascribed to a choice on his part and which she immediately liked for its humility.

"Bethanne's been experimenting with Sri Lankan," he said, bringing a big bowl of orange-coloured curry to the table. "When she's home, that is—you guys know all about that." Then later, "We probably should have gone out to eat. Nothing special here! Not like you get on the road." He seemed to be speaking to the bowl, which he continued to hold by its porcelain handles.

"Luke wants to make an animated feature. He has a character in mind," said Bethanne in her loud, eager voice.

Luke looked up, directly at Mélanie. His eyes seemed to apologize to her—for the childishness of his occupation? She couldn't tell. She had no judgment about animation except that she preferred live action. She could easily imagine this man spending all day sketching some kind of slouching, funny-sad figure that hadn't yet jelled, then feeling ashamed for it. Without knowing anything about him, Mélanie felt as if she could understand his private defeats, and so the look Luke gave her made her want to leave the house immediately because she could not hide her empathy. Luke didn't seem to care that Bethanne saw them sharing a moment. He kept on looking.

It became a ritual, Bethanne inviting Kassandra and Mélanie over for dinner whenever they were off the road. Like orphans. They'd get a phone call early in the day. Then Kassandra would pick Mélanie up in her Civic and it would normally be a Saturday, around seven o'clock. Kassandra was also at loose ends when she wasn't touring. She expressed this by acting sullen and drinking too much wine, as Bethanne did, which meant Mélanie would have to drive Kassandra's car home later and cab it back to her own apartment. She didn't mind. She didn't go to Bethanne's to drink with them or to try one of Bethanne's experiments with world cuisine. She went to see Luke.

Sometimes he would pick fights with Bethanne during these evenings, pestering her about recording her own album. She'd say she wasn't ready, that for the time being they needed her income. And why was he discussing this in front of her friends? Mélanie would tug at Kassandra's sleeve and claim she was tired, that they should go. "No, don't," Luke would say, putting up his elegant hand in a stop gesture. "We want you here." Mélanie knew he meant he wanted her there. Other times, he would touch her. Passing her on the way out of the kitchen. Getting up from the couch and pushing past her knees. The little touches that men risk, that make everyone nervous, but not quite enough to say anything about. Once, he beat Bethanne to the door and held it open for Mélanie as she was leaving. When everyone noticed, Mélanie wished she could come up with a joke to break the tension. But she didn't and left feeling embarrassed and excited.

One night, on a six-stop gig they did in Washington State and northern California, Mélanie visited Bethanne's room. Bethanne had just gone down the hall to the vending machine to grab a Mr. Goodbar and a Whatchamacallit—their favourite American chocolate bars. While she was gone, the phone rang. It was Luke.

"Bethanne's out."

He didn't say anything back. They breathed silently together. It was a conversation of a kind.

Then Bethanne opened the door and saw Mélanie with the receiver. She stood in the door, her bulky, heavy-boobed upper body heaving. For a moment Mélanie thought Bethanne would slam the door shut and storm down the hotel corridor. Instead, she reached out her hand in much the same self-assured way as she did onstage and began to walk forward. Mélanie handed over the receiver, got up, went back to her own room and covered her head with the bedsheets.

During shows, nothing seemed different. Bethanne stood between Mélanie and Kassandra as coloured lights swept over them in waves. Pink. Blue. Violet. When Bethanne stepped forward, Mélanie and Kassandra stepped forward too. It was like a code, one that unlocked the exuberance stored away in all three. Bethanne tapped this code out over and over. When she dropped, almost to her knees, and snaked back up, or twirled in place, flinging both arms into the air like branches to accentuate the end of a song, so did the other two. Kassandra's skin looked midnight dark onstage. Mélanie's long hair caught the light and glistened. But it was Bethanne who led, and she glowed from head to heel.

There were some differences during their transits from city to city. Bethanne found reasons to sit with Kassandra on the bus. At the hotel, after shows, Mélanie would walk by Kassandra's room and hear Bethanne laughing, Kassandra chuckling along, sometimes to the sound of a bottle being pulled from an ice bucket; friends conspiring over a nightcap. These changes worried Mélanie. She slept less. It took more and more energy to stay in tune with the singer-songwriter's music and with the tour as a whole.

Then they were home again. A two-week break. They arrived in the morning off the tour bus. Mélanie unpacked in the cramped studio apartment she'd rented after leaving her furnished room. It was winter and cold rain fell, icy and heavy, against the single-pane glass windows. She spent so little time in her own place, it was as though she'd never been there before. She sat down on the hard couch and drank a glass of water in the silent, bare room.

The idea came into her head suddenly, like it had been a message floating through the air that she happened to overhear. She rose from the couch with purpose. She took the bus across town, got off and walked through the rain. For a moment, standing outside, she felt the same interdiction against entering that the choir director must have felt that night she called him to say goodbye; this was not a house she was welcome in. But she also felt the thrill she'd experienced sitting near that grand fountain across from the management company's offices, only minutes to go before her interview. He opened the door wearing shorts because his and Bethanne's house was always overly hot and dry. She walked by him and the door shut quietly. There was nothing else. The world was a big, empty sound, like the moment Mélanie knew well from being onstage, when she and Bethanne and Kassandra would hold their second-last note for a long moment and the entire theatre would fill with anticipation before they cut it sharply. In that brief silence there was always another kind of music, a composed quiet just before the final, hard note washed in. That's what it was like with Luke that day, the two of them alone in Bethanne's house.

Bethanne must have suspected almost right away—maybe intuited it. They played three local shows. Big ones. Mélanie noticed a tremor in her fingers as she buttoned her dress and did her makeup before taking the stage. Her body wanted to be in transit. He had those hands. He told her everything. She had also said things to him. Not everything, but some of it. More than she'd told anyone else.

Onstage, the songs and dance moves began to feel disjointed, went from fluid to hinged. Mélanie felt that at any moment Bethanne might unhook her from the next sequence like a trailer from a travelling car, and she would roll down the hill and be lost. Her voice was unsteady. After the second show, the singer-songwriter came and told all three of them to get their act together, but it was Mélanie whom she glared at with her narrow eyes.

Another unexpected tour stop came up when the singer-songwriter developed laryngitis. They were off for three Saturdays. On the second of these, Kassandra called and said she'd be over to pick Mélanie up and take her to Bethanne and Luke's.

"Did they call?" said Mélanie. She sounded panicked because she was. "I don't remember them saying we were invited."

"If that'd stopped us before, we'd all be ten pounds lighter. Now get yourself ready and I'll be over in an hour to get you. I'm picking up the wine."

As soon as Bethanne opened the door, Mélanie knew. "We shouldn't have come," she said.

Bethanne looked tired, had been crying. Her big shoulders sloped sadly. Kassandra put a hand firmly over each, said "I'm here," then went to take off her coat. Bethanne turned to follow her and Mélanie understood that she had the option of running. But she could not. And so the three singers went down the hall, as if onto a stage, but really just into the living room where Luke was sitting on the hardwood floor. He had his elbows on his knees and his head down between his long hands. Kassandra shook her head at him and went to take a seat, but Bethanne grabbed her by the arm before she had the chance and pulled her into the kitchen, leaving Mélanie and Luke alone.

"I've told her everything," Luke said after a moment, not looking up. "I've told her we're in love and she'll have to let me go. You can't plan this kind of love, I said. You can't look for it. And she knows. I'm never in a hurry. She knows. But I'm hurrying now. I want you to leave the tour. I can't stand you being away."

Mélanie could hear mumbling from Bethanne and Kassandra just behind the kitchen door. She looked at Luke's hands and his little boy's kneecaps and was unable to speak.

Then Kassandra and Bethanne came back in and stood shoulder to shoulder as they did during shows. Mélanie noticed that Bethanne had spilled something on her blouse. Some kind of sauce. "Will you leave for him?" Bethanne asked her. "Will you?

That's what he wants." Her voice was even. It was as if she was asking about something impersonal, like Mélanie was a salesperson and Bethanne wanted to know if she would take back the shirt she had stained. She had big drops coming out of her eyes, but her detached tone made it difficult to understand them as tears. Mélanie didn't recognize this impersonal tone in her friend. Maybe Bethanne really did want to know what would happen so she could keep arranging things, for herself and Luke, maybe even Mélanie. Bethanne couldn't stop herself from leading.

Mélanie hesitated before answering. It wasn't right, the way this had come out. Luke didn't understand how good it felt to keep moving, to follow the order of things, how Bethanne had sewed everything together for her along the way. She worried she might come apart right then and there. She hugged herself.

Her troubled silence seemed to startle Luke. "Did you lie?" he blurted out, his voice shrill. "Can you stand there and tell me we shouldn't stay here together? I know we should. You told me those things, about your home town and that man."

She did love him. She had never even thought about anything coming up beside her singing, her job, or Bethanne's friendship like a competitor, running alongside, taking away her focus. He had caught her by surprise. Mélanie remembered something a therapist had once told her. This was before she'd ever sent in the demo tape, after her father had decided, six years too late, that something was wrong about Mélanie's relationship with the choir director, and had gone to stand in the man's garage with a .30–30 across his chest until the choir director came up the driveway. The police had been called. Eventually, the choir director had dropped the charges, but a guidance counselor at Mélanie's high school had arranged for some sessions with a therapist who visited the town's public health office once a month. Mélanie dreaded the idea and arrived purposely late for her first appointment. The therapist didn't scold her for this. She had the same relaxed, wait-and-see quality that Mélanie would later find in the steakhouse hostess. Mélanie planned to say nothing about the choir director, just as she had said nothing to the police, or to her father. But after a few sessions, when the therapist asked about the relationship and whether it was still happening, Mélanie nodded. Still later, the therapist asked if Mélanie felt like she'd lost herself in this relationship. When Mélanie nodded to that, too, the woman said, "It happens." She also said that if you lose part of yourself, it takes time to retrieve it. She suggested they discuss how Mélanie could do that. Was there anyone she trusted? Mélanie said that her best friend was her younger brother. So the therapist had proposed that Mélanie foster that friendship. In friends, she said, we can find pieces of ourselves.

Mélanie remembered all of this and then spoke for the first time since arriving at Bethanne's. "I have to leave," she said. Luke covered his face with one hand and wouldn't look at her. So she walked to the entrance, put on her coat and opened the door. When she had gone a full two blocks without anyone coming after her, she used her phone to call a cab and stood waiting for it, the toes of her rain boots disappearing into a muddy puddle.

Their next show was in Calgary. They flew coach, as always, waving as they passed by the singer-songwriter, now recovered, who was sitting in a wide business-class seat, drinking a glass of wine before the plane even took off. During rehearsals, the set-up was the same as usual: Kassandra on the right, Bethanne in the middle, Mélanie on the left. Bethanne wore a sequined minidress and her thighs shimmered in sheer hose. But she seemed less brilliant than usual, her light turned down, or like someone had pricked her and some composing element had leaked out. Inwardly, Mélanie calculated how many more moves until the night would be over.

Then, during the upbeat third song of the set, one of the singer-songwriter's best known, Bethanne started to pick up the pace, doing the kind of things backup singers do to keep each other interested. Things the audience isn't aware of. She was pushing Kassandra's range and Mélanie's nerves. She stepped forward and shifted left, normally an indication that they would do a quick revolve of positions. Kassandra went behind and up the middle first, singing. Even as Mélanie's mind and body and vocal cords worked to keep up, she was impressed by Kassandra's long-legged poise. Behind the lights, the front rows reacted with applause. Kassandra had found her point in the distance and they wanted to go where the music seemed to be taking her. Then Bethanne stepped centre and to the other side and it was Mélanie's turn to go up the centre. She came forward as she had done many times before, but when she found herself there, something about Bethanne and Kassandra's body language was wrong. It was like she had become trapped in fast waters between islands. If she looked, Bethanne's smiling profile would be there, she knew, but she wouldn't be guiding her. So Mélanie didn't look. She sang into her headset, and the music, the stage, everything began to fall away. No one was leading her. She tapped her hip with one hand and imagined, again, the choir director in the front row, watching, reprimanding. Then she couldn't tap out her beat any-more and she couldn't see Kassandra or Bethanne at all, because they'd each taken a step back. This was not part of the routine. Green and gold lights swept over her in rapid succession. The song was building towards its climax. Mélanie felt otherworldly, utterly alone. She carried out a series of steps that she knew by heart, each coming out unsteadily. As she executed the last move, her knees gave out and she felt herself tilt backwards in a dead fall for what seemed like a long time. Above her, the green and gold eyes of the lights blinked and swept away on their pivots.

Then two arms, hard like boards, landed against her lower back and pushed her forward and she was back standing, her breath knocked out of one long note. Bethanne got directly be-hind her and almost walked into her before Mélanie understood that she should move aside and resume her normal position. The show went on. There were two encores.

Afterwards, in the dressing room, Mélanie stepped up to the mirror where Bethanne was removing her makeup and stood behind her shoulder. "I should've walked off when you switched me like that. I should've left you guys there."

"You wouldn't have."

"It won't happen. Between me and him. I'm leaving."

"If you do, you're stupider than you look. Stupider than anyone thought."

But Mélanie did leave, told the singer-songwriter she'd had enough of tour buses and crews, set-ups and teardowns, and that her vocal cords were wearing out. They knew each other so little that the singer-songwriter took her at face value. The management company cut Mélanie a cheque and that was that; they didn't want to assign her elsewhere.

Mélanie tried teaching singing. But occupying the role that the choir director had always played with her was disastrous. She became depressed and had to abandon her first batch of students after three months. That's when she turned to waitressing. She had done occasional catering for an aunt's business during high school. She'd never minded service work, even liked the combination of chaos and clarity it involved. She left Vancouver and tried Nelson, where she got her first job, then moved to Kamloops and Penticton before coming back to the coast, where she felt less lost. It was almost a year after that when she got a call from her former landlord, who told her he had some of her mail. Among the junk and old bills she found Luke's letter. She resisted opening it for a long time. When she did, she felt that she could touch his hands through that paper, and in her mind she and Luke did feel each other through it. The experience reawakened the exact sensation Mélanie had had on the first day, standing in front of Bethanne's grimy house in a state of fear and desire. She didn't reply.

A year later, she ran into Kassandra, who was the same as always. She told Mélanie that Bethanne was pregnant and that she and Luke had moved to a better house. Bethanne was recording an album. Kassandra paused after relaying this summary. She continued to look away or towards the ground, but her face eventually softened, and she sighed. "Who knows how any of that will turn out? They're both a little cuckoo sometimes, if you ask me." Mélanie, who had rarely experienced intimacy with Kassandra, could tell this was an offering. She touched her former colleague's arm in gratitude. Then Mélanie thought of Bethanne's pregnant profile, how she would be coding again, with her useful body and her good lungs, and how she would never let that baby fall, would always have an arm there to grab it, and also how there wasn't any way things might have turned out differently except that Mélanie might have been less sorry, less inclined to leave her singing behind, like some people leave behind an exotic pet because it's too hard to maintain while they keep on going their own way, just as though they've never had such a beautiful thing at all.

AN OVERNIGHT
BUSINESS TRIP

Peter doesn't see any reason to hurry to his window seat, though they're preparing for takeoff and he once loved surveying the tarmac, enjoyed watching the luggage carriers dart under the belly of the plane, scrutinizing them with the hopes of seeing his own suitcase, proof that he was a person who went places. He would count the accordion-like airport bays within view, their mouths flopping open, and think of all the people they fed on daily. He even checked other taxiing jets for someone else sitting in a window like his, staring back. If he'd ever caught the eye of such a person, he would have waved. It took years, actually, for the thrill of these things, the charge he got from being in airports and airplanes, from cordoned-off areas and scanners, pull-down shades and headsets, to completely wear off.

"Good meeting, I hope?' It's the head steward, a man Peter has seen on this flight many times. He has paused from his job of closing overhead bins on his way through business class. Though he always engages Peter, his manner remains so formal that Peter is never sure the steward recognizes him.

"Excellent," says Peter.

"You had good weather, too. It's been horrible up there." The steward shivers with disgust as he tilts his head towards an imagined Vancouver, where they're headed.

"It's not so bad."

"But it's nearly May!" the steward pleads. He has told Peter that he hates the weather in his home city. It really seems to upset him—the topic comes up every time they speak. Peter is always surprised that rain can be such a preoccupation to someone who spends his days riding above the dreariness, all year long, and then in and out of airports, where the climate suits everyone. Peter tries to think of something else he should say to cheer the steward up, but the moment passes, and the steward smiles and moves along. *Click*, go more overhead bins at regular intervals beneath his confident hand. The steward carries out the minutiae of his job like it gratifies him to do so, Peter thinks, like a piano player who can never just tickle the ivories, whose fingers have to come down on each key, on every occasion, with a satisfying degree of purpose.

Someone touches Peter's shoulder and he realizes he's holding up a line of passengers. He sits and, uninterested in the activities outside, picks up the in-flight magazine. An ad for an LA hotel immediately makes him regret it. He knows he was just in that very building, two hours ago, but he can't remember anything about the room, can't picture himself in the shower earlier in the morning or riding the elevator down to the lobby or placing his keycard on the desk. Everything was the same as it's been so many times.

He puts the magazine away and looks around. Many of the people seating themselves in business class are like him. Flying for work. Blasé to the details of boarding. But they seem more relaxed than him, as if they are, despite it all, enjoying aspects of the routine. Peter envies them. This commute to LA is the boss's idea. Peter attends a monthly half-day "get-together" here because the rest of the employees at his level attend. Except they all live in California, while he runs the company's smaller outpost in Canada. The boss says the get-togethers (he won't let anyone call them "meetings") are about inclusion, and that Peter deserves, as much as the others, to experience how much fun work can be. And so, another round trip and hotel to add to Peter's regular travel schedule.

Mostly, the get-togethers mean golf. Occasionally, they involve motivational speakers. Once, they went zip lining. Peter clapped palm over palm atop the sliding mechanism that held him to the line, and his stomach flip-flopped as he sank at great speed into a dry ravine, convinced he would fall to the bottom and die there. He didn't, but was gripped with extreme vertigo. As he finally approached the platform at the other end, there was his boss, twisting and turning in Peter's deranged vision, but very much present, standing beside their guide. Peter knew that no matter how miserable he felt, he should smile. Like all the get-togethers, the zip was a show of power by the boss, a test Peter had no intention of failing. As soon as the guide had grabbed hold of his harness, he reached out and, concentrating all of his attention, found the boss's hand. "What a feeling," he managed to say. The boss seemed touched by these words and helped him unhook from the line. It was the closest they'd ever come, physically.

Now the boss has taken to complementing these types of events with social media. For example, all employees are supposed to interact through a company Facebook group—no shoptalk allowed. From the beginning Peter visited the group first thing every day to study other people's posts. At first he mimicked their safe contributions, posting viral cat videos and quizzes. Then he noticed a pattern: the boss regularly "liked" the smattering of overtly personal comments that were posted. The riskier the better. And so, when, on a warm afternoon in March, Peter took his assistant to lunch to celebrate her five years with the company, he tested himself, posting the image of the two of them sitting on a patio on Granville Island toasting with a glass of wine. He captioned it "Finalizing quarterlies." Within the hour, the boss "liked" the pic. Peter should have been pleased; he had discovered another of the invisible steps he had to climb for the sake of his career. But the process exhausted him, literally forcing him to bed early that evening. It seemed like the more he produced the emotion the company wanted from him, the less he felt for everything else.

The steward is back. He reaches for the bin directly above Peter's row, exposing the shiny, well-worn underarm of his uniform jacket. Then he pastes on a smile and moves along. How does he continue to care about these tasks? Peter puzzles over this question, all the while praying that the seat beside his will remain empty, so he can be alone with his thoughts.

The door has still not been closed. As usual, there is some delay. Peter considers the weirdness of flight. Tidily arranged strangers in a great tube of steel. A memory floats to him from his childhood in the small Northern Ontario town where his father was an electrician. There was no airport there, of course. But planes passed daily over their house, and Peter can see again the white trails they would draw against the sky, which started out sharply white, but which would go blurry after the plane was gone. Peter always found this sad. They had gone, left so little, as though his place in the world deserved only the afterthought. He can remember, too, his mother calling him in for supper, the warm sound of his parents' voices as they conversed quietly over their Scrabble board. They died much too early.

A passenger appears at the top of the aisle. She must be the one holding things up. It's a woman Peter sees nearly every month. Tall, with an extra-straight back, like she's always about to make a speech. She wears a long, light camel's hair coat. She is about his age, maybe older. The steward, who once caught Peter looking at her, has told him with a raised brow that she's a senior executive. Never married. She has a self-assured demeanour Peter finds intimidating. Everyone in the business section stares at her, and not only, he thinks, because they have nowhere else to look. She has presence. The steward greets her warmly, with zero irritation at her lateness, checks her ticket stub and shows her to her seat—the aisle seat in Peter's row. The steward relieves the executive of her expensive-looking carry-on and stores it in the overhead bin, then touches her sleeve meaningfully, as if to say, "I'll make this as painless as possible for you." He can be obsequious that way, Peter thinks, at the same time wondering why he has not been similarly fawned over. The woman ducks her head to sit down and smiles at Peter. He can't tell whether the smile is one of recognition or not, whether he should feel regretful that she's disturbed his peace.

"Warm in here, isn't it?" she says. She folds up her luxurious coat and rests it in the space between their seats, revealing her fitted black turtleneck and soft-looking cream pants. As she crosses her legs, he also makes out the exotic-looking heel of a black boot.

"Let's be kind and call it spring air."

"Let's," says the executive, smiling. "Thank goodness for spring."

"Yes. Definitely. Thank goodness. I love spring. Especially in Vancouver. Everything just comes alive." Peter says these things without being sure where they come from, like the smile and handshake he produced for his boss after zip lining. They are standardized responses. They cover his bases, the way that hotel he stayed in offers standardized comfort. Both keep people from asking too many questions. Yet, as he often does, Peter flashes to an image of his father listening to this banter, stone-faced, and he has to physically shake the thought away.

The executive doesn't notice. As they finally taxi towards the runway, she bends forward to tug a document and her glasses from the sleek leather briefcase she has stowed under the seat ahead of her. She looks at ease as she begins to read, like she was born to be here, doing just this work. Peter cannot help but resent her, as he has grown to resent many others who have been given so much—looks, style, a way with the world—when they are probably undeserving, no better than anyone else, maybe worse. His own life has been so much work. He has come up a cliff, in his own mind, from the abyss of his childhood. The worst possible thing for someone like him would be to fall in love at this point in his life. This last idea catches him by surprise. He is not in love with this stranger! He nearly laughs out loud at the contents of his mind. He glances again at the woman, who has opened her briefcase once more and pulled out an iPad. Peter glances at the steward. Is this a breach of protocol during take-off? But the steward is at the front of the cabin, acting out the safety procedures, arms swaying perfectly towards hard stops and back to his sides. He does not seem to notice the executive's iPad, and she, in turn, doesn't seem concerned about scolding. Perhaps the steward has allowed this before, a concession Peter knows he could not expect. The executive is polite about it. She pauses with her clean hands holding the paper document on top of the iPad, waiting for the captain to extinguish his sign and grant her permission to turn the device on, like a girl waiting with a beloved book. Peter finds this erotic and shifts in his seat.

The plane breaks before moving abruptly forward again, increasing its speed for takeoff. As it does, Peter notices something wrong with his chair back. It has sunk away from the upright position. He struggles with the lever, even as it dawns on him that the small TV screen embedded into the seat ahead of him has not been playing back the safety video. He fiddles with it, but the screen won't turn on. He fumes inwardly. He enjoys watching a movie on the way home from the LA trip. There will be a hill of work to face back at the office, and this is his break time. He considers changing spots but cannot bring himself to ask the steward to reassign him to a TV-friendly seat with the executive within earshot. He'll seem so childish. He stays quiet but feels foiled.

When they finally leave the ground, Peter does experience a glimmer of excitement. Something sparks as the rumble of wheels ceases. He momentarily senses the outer edge of that old thrill. And he might be able to keep it in focus, he thinks, if only his seat weren't tilting backwards. He distracts himself from the annoyance by looking out the window, as the city below takes on the aspect first of a puzzle, then of a microchip, hundreds of sprawling neighbourhoods reduced to pinpoints. He thinks about how small the company offices really are, and sees very clearly how insignificant and bullying his boss is. Peter has always feared being suspected as different, as though he married above his station by joining such a good boutique firm. He can't afford to take a stand on the get-togethers. Do his colleagues sense his dislike of the trip? Snicker behind his back?

Eventually, the steward comes around with drinks. As he reaches over with Peter's coffee, the plane drops altitude and some coffee spills onto Peter's good pants. "Shit!" he says, furious. "Goddamnit."

"I'm so sorry," says the steward, though his apology seems practiced. He hands Peter some extra napkins stamped with the airline's blue logo.

"Oh, dear," says the executive. She sounds more genuine. She offers Peter her own coffee.

"No, thank you. I'm fine," says Peter, regretting swearing. "Quick stop at my dry cleaners and I'll be good to go. They see me coming." He adds a laugh, trying to erase traces of his bad humour.

"Here you go," says the steward, handing Peter a fresh cup, around which he has somehow tied one of the napkins in an elegant triangle.

"Lovely," says Peter. The steward does things so well. Peter feels remorseful for his own self-pitying stance towards work. "Thanks."

"It's crazy, but I still like it," says the executive.

"What's that?"

She points out the window. "The view. Even after all this time."

Peter follows her finger, which is aimed at the cloud cover they are still rising through. Everything in sight is a shade of grey. Exactly as the snow would look from inside the tunnels he built every winter as a child, he realizes. He never did relish spring, which would melt his elaborate pathways, his private palaces, to nothing. He nods, but can't tell if the executive was joking. She turns back to her iPad, which Peter can see is equipped with a satellite uplink plug-in, and with which she is now reviewing some charts that must complement her paper document, shifting back and forth between them. After a moment, though, and with a long index finger, she pulls her charts off-screen to reveal her browser, opened to her Facebook page. Peter has to work not to stare. A seat away, yet it's as though they are flying through different dimensions. The executive navigates the personal and professional effortlessly, while he has found that, with the years, he is cannier, yes, but nothing more. There are no smooth transitions. In many ways he is alone, has had limited contact with people in his life. He no longer feels so hemmed in by a lack of money. But the adulthood he's achieved is circumscribed by the need to prove his worth. He is as confined by purpose as the green tabs of Californian farms are by lengths of highway surrounding them, a sight which he now glimpses through a break in the clouds.

And yet, what *about* this executive? She has her good clothes. Her certainty. What else has she got? Peter begins to doubt the sincerity of her friendliness—as he must, as others must doubt his. In that same conversation he once had about her with the steward, Peter learned that the executive had recently been named top earner by her company. Probably, Peter concludes, she is so arrogant she thinks she's untouchable. He looks over once more and notices that around the eyes the executive is quite thoroughly wrinkled. There might even be a downward curve at the mouth, despite it being painted a precise, even red. She is decaying, just a bit. How long do you get to be top earner? How good she must be at faking it! And for what? For money? Peter can almost see his father shaking his head. And thinking this, Peter feels desperate to be alone and has an urge, humiliating to him and also intense, to bump the executive with his elbow, rattle her cage. This makes him feel even more abjectly alone, his own potential for violence making him suddenly, illogically, feel that he must get up and stretch his legs.

"Excuse me," he says, standing as much as the overhead bin will allow. The executive gets up from her seat and lets him out. Peter notes that he is taller than she is. He goes down the aisle to the washroom and, once inside, sits down on the seat and rubs his hands together. He wishes he were already home. He will call his assistant when they land, tell her he's not feeling well. Then he can go by the delicatessen in his neighbourhood and buy himself prepared food, to the liquor store for a better-than-usual bottle of Scotch. He can download a film. He longs for these luxuries, for the spacious Yaletown apartment he will soon own outright. Conjuring them fills Peter with relief that he does not live the suffocating workaday life his parents lived. He's made it.

When he returns to his seat, the executive stands again. They face each other for a moment. "Did you manage to get the coffee off?" she says, eyeing him. Can she read his thoughts, Peter wonders, wishing he could erase the jumbled contents of his mind.

"What? And deny my dry cleaners a visit? How could I?"

She smiles, but looks tired by his jokes. "You're on this flight a lot, I guess."

"Yes. You too?"

"Yes. Often."

In the seats across from them, two female business travellers, quite a bit younger, break into laughter at some private joke. The executive turns towards them, scrutinizes them a moment. They bring down their voices, as though chastised, and yet with a camaraderie that seems to purposely exclude their older counterpart. When she turns back to Peter, the executive's face seems different—distressed, regretful for something lost, maybe. There could be an overture here, Peter thinks. He could touch her lightly, in a friendly but manly fashion, rescue her from their judgment by acknowledging her stature. But he isn't sure—can't be—that she would want that.

The executive brings a smile to her face.

"Well," says Peter, afraid to embarrass her by holding her gaze for too long. He steps past her and takes his seat.

When their descent begins, Peter does up his seat belt and rests his newspaper so that it touches the executive's coat between their seats. Something about this arrangement comforts him, as if someone could come down the aisle now and think he and she were a couple unconsciously letting their things—a nice coat, a serious newspaper, an expensive tablet—clutter casually together. A moment later though, the steward comes by and plucks the newspaper away, asks them to stow their belongings. He bequeaths wide smiles onto both his regulars and moves on.

The plane arcs downwards. The land outside the window explodes back to size and Peter feels more real again, as though he is being drawn from a dream. It is brilliantly sunny over Vancouver. The cherry trees have blossomed and pink lines of them are drawn everywhere. Peter realizes he's been counting on quieter, less vibrant weather—the kind the steward nodded towards. Thoughts of his apartment evaporate and Peter craves the imminent reunion with his desk. When they come to a full stop and the sound of seat belts unbuckling fills the cabin, the executive says goodbye and gathers up her things. On the ramp outside the plane door she moves off quickly, her coat tails scissoring open and closed, her cream pant legs moving lightly over the good boots, and disappears.

It is in the Arrivals area, behind the long elastic barrier where people wait to greet family and friends, that Peter sees someone familiar. The same gentle demeanour as his father. A person who carries his working man's logic everywhere with him like a carry-on, though he goes nowhere. The man appears confused. He might be in the wrong waiting area, or the person he's come to meet is missing, or his mind might be slipping. For a moment Peter remembers, exactly as it was, his family's kitchen in the late morning when he was a boy. His mother would make her own bread. His father would eat nearly half a loaf of it with butter while it was still warm. The kitchen would smell like baking for hours. Visualizing the room, smelling it again, Peter, standing with his overcoat and bag, feels a great love rise up in his chest—as though he might be taken right up off the ground. And he almost says, aloud, the term of affection his parents always used for him. But then the man turns, unexpectedly, and goes. Peter walks along the barrier, the wheels of his suitcase rolling smoothly on the endless blue carpet, past all the eager faces of people who wait for others.

NO POWER

She is suddenly awake, consciousness like a screen lighting up, a rough-cut version of their afternoon on playback. What shows there shocks her. She squeezes her eyes shut and open again. The room is silent, lit the gold of early evening, the air is still and oppressively hot, and she is sweaty.

He gets up first, limps down the hall to his bathroom. When he returns, he is that different person she also knows. He wants her out. "What time is it?" he says, looking at his bare wrist, then rooting around aggressively for his watch.

"It's late," she says, helpfully. "I'd better take off."

Franklin seems scattered. He abandons his watch search almost before it's begun and looks around the room as though trying to tell if it really is the one he normally shares with his wife. "Something's wrong with the central air," he says, walking over to the temperature control. Nicole can see he is sore.

She picks herself up off the bed. She doesn't have any bruises that she can see. "Your clock's off too," she says, staring into the dead face of the bedside alarm.

"Huhn," he says, but he's distracted again. He is hauling the sheets off the bed and balling them up. As if his wife will be home any moment. As if he needs to neutralize the damage. They both know she doesn't fly back until tomorrow morning.

It's Nicole's turn to go down the hall to the bathroom. She flicks on the light switch. Nothing happens. She leaves the door slightly ajar, letting in some natural light from the hall windows. Sitting on the toilet, naked, she wonders how long this business with Franklin can go on, and is unnerved because she can't see the end.

When she gets back to the bedroom, he is standing beside the sheets, which have liberated themselves, despite him. He has puffed himself up the way she's seen him do many times when dealing with contractors, his glasses returning to him, now, some of the authority of his job. But from the head down he looks like a boy, not an architect. He has thrown on the first thing he found in his dresser drawer—a yellow T-shirt and faded red shorts. He looks at her as if to say, "Where are *your* clothes?"

"Power's out," he says instead.

"No kidding. Guess we blew a fuse, baby."

"I hope to God we won't lose a fridge full of food," he says, ignoring her, and like whatever is in the kitchen represents the last rations he and his wife will be allotted.

"That would suck."

"Look, Nic, I . . ."

"Please shut up," she says, her back turned, pulling on her skirt. "We'll have coffee at work tomorrow."

"Okay. Sure. Yeah," he says, his voice looser now, confirming something to himself. "I just gotta get this mess cleaned up." Nicole can't see his face, but is sure it has been recalibrated to contrition. On that same screen in her mind, she sees Franklin, fifteen minutes from now, on his knees again, stuffing every shred of evidence into the washer, doubling the detergent.

She buttons up her rumpled work shirt, thanks God she had the foresight to keep a hair elastic around her wrist, and looks into Franklin's wife's mirror, where she adjusts herself as best she can. She will never be pretty. It's just a fact. She has made peace with her nose, however. Franklin hovers, silently hurrying her. She defies him, taking the time to straighten her suit jacket, wishing she still smoked so that she could make him suffer more, pollute his sanctuary—pollute herself in it. Instead she says goodbye. Music to his ears. She receives a dry consolation kiss on the forehead and is escorted to the back door, no last look at the front entrance where she first pinned him against the wall. She thinks, *I'm being recycled*, but reminds herself that this is part of the bargain and that she entered into it freely.

Outside, the heat takes her in its grip and she is jarred, disoriented, but glad; it makes her feel sane. She has a six-block walk to the subway, during which she can also recalibrate. She wants her face to read uninvolved, unknowing. The heat will help her sweat out the rest.

All the houses she passes look like Franklin's. His neighbours have a knack for arrogant entranceways. Many have stone vases on the front step that hold imposing, competitive arrangements of flowering plants. Cast in deepening evening shadow, this could be a row of funeral parlours. Nicole remembers the countless cheery drawings of her dream home that she made as a child. Most were painted mint green, her favourite colour, or in stripes. A waterslide would always be spiraling down from some upstairs window—the quickest way to her heart-shaped pool. Later, she got secretive, struggling to depict a plain building whose inner walls, all made of glass, faced a secret courtyard, complete with play gym for a pet monkey, of course. There are no hidden monkeys on Franklin's street.

She is preoccupied enough with such judgments that it is only when she finally gets to Yonge and Lawrence that she realizes something odd is going on. The stores she passes all have makeshift signs saying, "CLOSED. NO POWER." Outside the subway station, people are scuttling around like ants disturbed from their hole. Nicole goes past them to the turnstiles.

"Trains aren't running, Miss," a TTC worker says, looking exasperated, refusing eye contact as Nicole approaches. "Haven't been since late afternoon."

"What's going on?" Nicole asks, but the worker has already turned around and is advancing toward some older women, waving her arms at them in a "Don't bother!" gesture.

Nicole walks back out to the bright street corner where, squinting at the scene, she sees a man in a sweat-soaked work shirt directing traffic. He clearly has no idea what he is doing. Traffic is bunching up in every direction. As she watches, a woman gets out of her car and hands him a child's twirling baton, but it is pink and sparkly and just makes him look eccentric as well as inept. People start to honk, and Nicole gets the feeling that much has transpired since she left the office with Franklin at three o'clock for the site survey that never happened. That turned into a caution-to-the-wind stop at a liquor store. Which became drinks and fondling on a park bench. Which, in turn, became twin conspiratorial cellphone calls to cancel their late meeting with the senior project coordinator, ending with she and Franklin driving, too drunk, the short distance to his house. Though they have not courted, have not assumed the nitty-gritty regularity of picking times and places, and have never discussed their complementary approaches to pleasure, still, somehow, every so often, they hear a single, fervent thought pass between them: opportunity. They take it. He gives her control. She uses it. They fit. But only that way. Briefly.

"You need water?" someone says to her now.

"Excuse me?"

"Water. Four bucks a pop. If you're one of them that's walking home—you're gonna need water."

"I'll take a taxi, thank you."

"No cabs. You'll be walkin'," says the woman, as though pronouncing a sentence. Nicole dislikes her voice and her chinless face. Maybe this registers, because the woman turns and plods away with her two big bags full of bottled water. The ass of her flood-length khakis is dark with perspiration.

Walk home? Nicole feels dizzy at the very idea. She needs a shower. She might still be just a bit drunk. And she is thirsty. Parched. "Actually, wait," she calls to the woman, "I'll take one—please." The woman turns and pulls out one small, lukewarm Evian. Nicole pats her side and realizes: her purse—she's left it at Franklin's. An electric tingle travels up from her feet. "I don't have any money," she says, more to herself than to the woman.

"Sorry to hear that."

Furious with herself, wanting the water very badly, and trying to determine whether Franklin will be kind enough to resist burning her things before his wife gets back, Nicole riffles through her satin-lined suit pockets.

"Another one who lives by the almighty credit card, Interac—whatever else is plastic," says the woman, shaking her head.

Nicole pretends not to hear and manages to locate, finally, a crumpled twenty-dollar bill. She proffers it, but the woman waves it off. "This heat'll do you in. Shouldn't be out without any ID or change during a power outage." She hands Nicole a free water. As she does, her eyes shift in a way that indicates she has received payment of a different kind, having seized her chance to chastise. It should not, Nicole thinks, feel like such a bad deal, but it does.

Still, unwilling to persuade this woman to take her last bill, Nicole lumps it. She opens her water bottle and drinks its contents in one long series of gulps, then looks around. Among the many people at the intersection, she makes out a steady flow of business people walking north. But they can't all be walking up from downtown! Nicole lives on the waterfront. It will take hours. Looking west down Lawrence, she feels a kind of panic tighten in her stomach. Her hair has begun to extract itself from the elastic and flutters around her face, getting caught at the edge of her lips and making her nose itch. She pushes it back and glares around her. It is as if the street has become part of a foreign city, and she a disoriented, clueless tourist who doesn't know the language. She begins to crave, doubly, the comfort of home. It's the first place Nicole has ever lived that isn't a rental. As a teenager, it was always her job to decorate whatever apartment she and her mother occupied. Cans of paint, cheap candles and throws— she came to despise them all, eventually rejecting the whole idea of cosmetic upgrades and dreaming instead of taking a mallet to old drywall, of tearing out cracked linoleum. Which is why no one can understand the un-renovated state of her little east-end bungalow. After one afternoon there together, Franklin all but ordered her to contract someone to do the job, but Nicole knew she wouldn't. That will be her pleasure, when she can afford it.

Her cell is, of course, at Franklin's with her bag, so she crosses back to the subway entrance, where a rare row of pay phones still stands. Ahead of each is a lineup ten people deep. As she waits, beads of sweat rolling down her stomach from under her breasts, Nicole overhears scraps of conversation that confirm what's started to dawn on her: ". . . says the whole city's out . . ."; ". . . people are still down there in the dark . . ."; ". . . afraid they'll be looted, so they're staying put." When she finally gets her turn at the tepid receiver, she can't seem to get through to Franklin's cell. She hefts the dangling phone book container to look for his home number, only to find the page she needs ripped out. She dials 411 but something is wrong with the line. She dials the operator and has the same problem. "No," she says, slamming down the receiver. "No. No. No." The people who've lined up behind her deflect her frustration like mirrors.

She considers walking back to Franklin's, but cannot imagine ringing his doorbell, finding him clean-shaven, changed into appropriate clothes, greeting her with—what? She can only imagine the kind of self-hate and indignation he might take out on her. He is, after all, the one with the wife, with seniority. He only likes to toy with the idea of vulnerability. Screw it, she thinks. Her things may as well be locked in a garrison. She'll start walking. She can pick up more water on the way. The concierge at her building will let her into her condo, and she can still get a good night's sleep. She must have candles somewhere. It will be fine.

She goes back to the corner and merges against the now very heavy northbound foot traffic, an eerie army of people who look just like her and Franklin, returning from offices probably much like her own. How grim, she thinks. But a few minutes in, as she finds a rhythm, she begins, uncharacteristically, to enjoy herself. It's absurd. The whole city really does seem to be without power. People are giving off an energy Nicole remembers from her childhood. Growing up, whenever the power went out, she would sing songs with her mother, and she would feel that anything was possible, that she could be anyone she wanted. It was ironic that in university, where she was finally given free reign, the feeling started to flicker out. While she and her classmates were encouraged to consider architecture in its broadest sense, she maintained a narrow interest in housing. She got into the trendy idea of repurposed building materials—intermodal containers, concrete, retrieved beams—but only for the possibilities they offered for designing homes that could be stacked or scattered, depending on the need, like Lego. Even as her models became more and more baroque, multiplying the options for rearrangement, she had the creeping feeling that recreating herself was impossible; her psychic parts seemed soldered together.

People are standing in the shadowy doorways of their flower shops, hair salons, and computer stores with nothing better to do, as if the pedestrians were part of a civic parade. Nicole overhears scraps of jokes and finds herself smiling at the corny punchlines. One man says all this unplanned exercise is very bad news for gyms, good news for shoe repairmen. Another woman tells everyone within earshot that she's been walking for three hours already and can't imagine what trouble her children are up to. There is only the slightest note of fear in her voice, and Nicole wishes she hadn't caught it.

As the sun sets and the comments continue, block upon block, Nicole feels sorry for them—these people whose need for drama has been met by a false, temporary emergency. By nightfall the power will have been restored and their lives will be as boring as when they'd plugged in their blow-dryers this morning. This is play-acting, just as it was when she was a child. Deep down, Nicole knows she can't be anyone but herself. In spite of the games she plays with Franklin, or maybe because of them, she does not believe in change. Soon this will be over. She will take the subway the rest of the way home. She will bathe and sleep and return to work and drink coffee beside Franklin. No harm done. Still, every so often, she reaches into her suit pocket and palms the twenty-dollar bill.

But when, more than an hour later, her feet have started to hurt, and she is wet with sweat, and it is pitch black, and the city has been sucked into an impenetrable abyss, and she is not quantifiably closer to home—when all her brief good humour and tolerance have been walked off—Nicole begins to resent the cheery, nearly festive mood of the crowd, the cars stuffed with young men who pass, hooting their horns in knuckleheaded fraternity, the friendly neighbours who share full glasses of water at street corners. People are actually *celebrating* this, she thinks with enough disgust to spit, though she never would.

Eventually she decides she can stand it no longer. She gets off Yonge Street and heads for the nearest residential street that parallels it to the west. There, she reasons, she can at least go about her trudging in peace. Two steps from the corner, though, darkness takes away her vision like a blindfold. She sees just glimmers of the occasional candle in a front window, like holes poked in black cloth. She has had so little experience with real darkness that her mind jumps to a night during her final year of university, during the spring term, when she had the unbelievable luck of studying in Rome. She and her classmates were given a special tour of the catacombs, the Christian-historian tour guide going so far as to cut the lights to allow them to stand in total darkness among the emptied, moist-smelling, oblong tombs, and truly experience the ancient choice of venue for the dead. Nicole had not felt afraid. Rather, she'd been envious of those early, persecuted believers, who'd had an entire underworld to reshape.

As she walks, Nicole is twice startled by people who come upon her from the opposite direction. She imagines, again, those stupid, morbid urns that must still be sitting on the steps of all the houses she's passing, just steps away. In the void she feels her usual certainties being worn down. Doubts about her choices. Her preferences. The darkness feels like it is seeping through her skin. She quickens her pace, tries to focus on the regular *click-click* of her heels.

Suddenly a woman appears out of the dark.

"Hello," the woman says, passing.

"Hi," says Nicole.

The woman stops: "Nicole?"

Then both women turn, coming very close, like dogs, to confirm each other's features, which appear grainy.

"Holy geez! I can't believe this!" says the woman, who turns out to be the rather too young and angular receptionist for the group of offices where Nicole works. "What are you doing here? Don't you live downtown?"

"Oh, yes. Um . . ."

"Isn't this *nuts*?" the woman jumps in. "Apparently, it's going to be out for days. I think I found the last Chinese takeout in the city for me and my husband!" she says, hoisting a greasy paper bag of food.

Nicole's throat has tightened. "I was on a site survey," she blurts out. "A site survey just north of here. I couldn't get home." She reaches up and touches her hair nervously. Then her soiled shirt collar.

The receptionist adopts a queer look. "Oh," she says. "You were on a survey all this time?" And Nicole can see, even through the inky darkness, something clarifying in the receptionist's clever, mouse-like eyes: she was the one who put through both Nicole's and Franklin's calls this afternoon.

"Well, I'll let you get back on your way, then," says the receptionist, evenly, and Nicole wishes she could hit this girl in her smug mouth.

"Yes, I'd better keep going."

They take three steps from each other and, when Nicole turns to get a last look, the receptionist has already disappeared, carrying her sweet-smelling Chinese and her secret irretrievably into the hot night.

At the next intersection, Nicole, stunned, and despite the intense pain in her feet, hurries back to the relative security of Yonge Street, where people have now formed a throng, a human mass she wants to disappear into. She continues her walk but calculates, with every step, how long it will take for the leak she's caused to spread. Another forty minutes and she's convinced she will be sunk by what will become known of her and Franklin. She passes a young man with a goofy face and a loose sandwich board that reads, "COLD ONE-DOLLAR PINTS TODAY ONLY!" Before she knows what she's done, Nicole has answered the call and steps past him into the bar.

It smells like a lifetime of stale beer, and she would normally be repelled. Instead she takes a seat at the bar, where they have placed candles at regular intervals, and orders the beer. All around her, groups of people, probably taking a break from their own long north- or southbound walks home, seem to be content to share the situation with strangers. The mood is giddy. From behind the bar comes the sound of ice being disrupted—stocked coolers, presumably. Nicole sits with her back to everyone, irritated, and sips her beer by candlelight. Even in architecture school she avoided this kind of spontaneous group intimacy. In the studio, when others really let go, becoming dramatic during late-night study sessions, making their emotional lives available to all through tears or hysterical laughter or PDAs, Nicole froze. It was like being forced to rifle through someone's garbage. She would've built herself a partition if it had been allowed. Instead, she sketched more and more. Smoked ceaselessly. And developed an interest in pulp imagery, then early pornographic photography. Most of this was an affectation; her school endorsed freaks. But those core aversions, and interests, stuck.

Now a very old woman approaches the bar. With great effort, she props her curved bird frame up on the stool next to Nicole and orders a whisky sour. In the flickering light, Nicole makes out her aristocratic profile, like a Rembrandt portrait. The woman turns to Nicole and considers her for a long moment with her deeply creased face. Just once. Thoroughly. Then a jolt of recognition turns some idea on, and one corner of the woman's mouth pulls up into an amused grimace, as though she is reading some aspect of Nicole's condition. Nicole knows better. There's nothing in her that isn't in everyone else. No stain.

But the woman keeps looking. "My dear," she says, in a voice like paper being crumpled, "you are lovely."

Nicole gets up. She has felt anything but lovely all day—for much longer. She is in no mood to be so badly misread. By a senile stranger, no less. But the old lady reaches into the substantial leather handbag on her lap and brings out a red case, holding it up to her. Inside are two long, heavy-looking cigarettes. "Electronic," says the woman, passing one to Nicole. "Try."

Impressed by her intuition, maybe feeling, after all, that the power outage has caused some break in her routine notions, Nicole lets herself reach in for one of the cigarettes. Smoking was once the ideal drawbridge between her and others, allowing her to decide, if only on that small scale, who got through, who was allowed to share her secrets. She inhales deeply, happily, nostalgically, her lungs filling with minty vapour. She blinks at the woman, who is busy digging out an alligator-skin change purse. She pinches from it a one-dollar coin, putting it down on the bar beside Nicole's pint. "Your ale is on me," she says, lifting her milky eyes so that two identical reflections of the candle's flame leap into them.

Nicole drags on her cigarette again, evaluating her worthiness of these kind gestures, considering the unlikelihood of being deemed lovely, here and now. She crosses her legs and lets herself feel it. Be it. Then she turns her gaze to the candle itself, which occupies a spot just beyond the woman's manicured but skeletal hand. There, in the flame's yellow heart, Nicole recognizes a malicious glare. She quickly, forcefully, attempts to blow it out. She blows and blows, but the flame only wavers. So, pinching her fingers around it, feeling the burn, she makes it go out.

THE MERMAID SINGS

The night of my sister's wedding, I stuff my bridesmaid's dress into the dumpster in the alley beside my apartment building. Stuck between garbage bags, it looks like a paper carnation. There is no way to stop its cheery, seafoam spirit. I let the dumpster lid go and make a decision: I will buy a wig and become a Joni Mitchell impersonator.

I quit my telemarketing job and withdraw my savings, such as they are. I ask a friend to move into my apartment for a while and he accepts. Having never really been anywhere, I walk to a public library and use Google Maps to find towns along the TransCanada Highway small enough to book an act like mine, then dig up the numbers for local hotels and bars. I make a series of calls. Using my trained telephone manner, I inform each person in charge that they will shortly receive a package including a headshot and audio file of "Joan-ey" Mitchell. In this way I have no trouble setting up a string of gigs.

I take the subway downtown and find the wig I need at a shop that also sells beaded curtains, bongs, old issues of *Heavy Metal*. At home I bend over, pull on the wig and stand up quickly, throwing the new hair back over my shoulders. It is long and acrylic, with plenty of bangs. I look at myself in my small, medicine-cabinet mirror, the short tube of light buzzing above me. It makes the wig almost white at the crown, my skin and eyes nearly grey. I don't stand there long.

I buy sheet music for all the Joni Mitchell songs I can find and spend a long time memorizing the lyrics. My phone rings often but I ignore it. I prepare my packages, mail them out, then write a note for my friend. He can relay the news to my family. I stuff my backpack with jeans and loose shirts, snap my guitar case shut, take a cab to the Greyhound station and buy a bottle of water, a cling-wrapped egg salad sandwich, and an open-ended cross-country ticket, westbound.

On the bus I claim a window seat. The sight of the disappearing city is dreary in bare late fall, but soon gold-brown farmers' fields, then rusty outcrops and pine trees take its place. The bus stops often to drop off packages and give the smokers a chance to rush down the metal steps and get some air. The person beside me keeps changing: an older Native woman who knits then nods, a university student wearing extra large earphones who stares at my wig, a skeleton-thin mother in faded jeans who bites her nails and ignores her four-year-old as he runs up and down the aisle.

"I'm a musician," I tell each of them. (The student has to pull up a headphone to hear me.)

"What kind of music?"

"Folk."

The Star Motel, in Gravenhurst, is my first venue. I've been offered free dinner and a room for the weekend, but no pay. I meet the manager at 6 p.m. In person, I am less confident than over the phone, and he eyes me over his bifocals—probably thinking I am too short and too dumpy to be Joni, or even Joan-ey. He says I'm lucky. A new-country trio bailed on him the day I called. We go over the set-up and he recedes into a dim back-room. I order chicken fingers and fries, finish my plate, then walk across the cigarette-burned carpet leading to my room. There, I make a single call and get the answering machine. "Hi, Mom. It's me. I'm sorry I've been out of touch and missed the gift opening and all the rest of it. . . but I had to get going. Don't worry. I've got something worked out for myself."

I am relieved to find only seven people in the audience when I step up onto the plywood stage. Two of them are older men who sit across from each other and ignore me. They lean together and regularly slap one another on the shoulder over their pitcher. One woman sits alone clutching a single beer bottle: Bud Light Lime. The others look like summer students who've been drink-ing since noon. The bartender paces in the long space behind the bar with a dishtowel over one shoulder, clinking glasses as she goes. I stand a moment, waiting for my courage. It arrives with the manager, who reappears from the backroom to lean on the bar, looking a little threatening.

The first song I play as Joan-ey is "Blue." Then "A Case of

You." Then the song I sang for my sister at her wedding. I recognize that my voice is wrong for Joni Mitchell covers. But the wig is right, and so are my jeans and bohemian cotton top. I smile as a few more people trickle in, and nearly all of them clap quietly as I finish my first set.

I have a better show in Sudbury and am paid for it. At the Canadian, in Sault Ste. Marie, I get too drunk on free draught and screw up the words to "Little Green." I apologize into the silver ball of the mic and the sparse audience gives me a staggered consolation clap before returning to their drinks. At the Whalen, in Thunder Bay, a drunk man shouts out, "Show us your tits!" but I don't. In Steinbach, Manitoba, the tiny Green Tree Café is full to capacity with people I later realize are Mennonites. They are my first sober crowd and stand and clap as I finish, even though I'm sure I have been off-key. A short woman in a long skirt approaches the corner that's been cleared for my footstool and mic to tell me I am beautiful. Mennonites really are generous.

That night, in my motel room, I dream of a wedding. It is a lot like my sister's wedding, but there are important differences. My sister, when she lifts her veil, is bald. Everyone is horrified. They turn together to find me, the maid of honour, wearing a seafoam dress and a blonde wig. I run, and the entire wedding party chases. I stumble and fall. I look up from the ground and find I have landed at the feet of Joni Mitchell. Joni's eyes shine like emeralds. With the power of her mind, Joni lifts me up. Then we are flying together over rolling hills made entirely of sheet music. Everything is Chagall-pretty. The dream wakes me. I am bathed in sweat. I take an extra-long shower and give my wig a thorough wash and blow-dry before checking out to re-board the Greyhound.

I sing in Carman. I sing in Brandon. And I sing in Moosomin. Between these gigs and the free chicken fingers, I save enough money to afford a day off. I book myself into a small inn in Wolseley, Saskatchewan. The bus drops me off in the early evening. The sun is already down. I follow directions and walk along a dark road then over the railroad tracks until I find it—a converted brick farmhouse with little white lights in the bushes outside. Classy. The girl at the desk asks about my guitar. I tell her I'm a musician and she smiles as though this explains a lot.

In my room there's no TV, so I walk down to the living room–sized basement pub. As I enter, everyone turns to stare, then go back to talking. On an overhead TV, *Tattoo Nightmares* is on, but no one is watching. The girl from the main desk comes downstairs into the pub and takes my order. I drink a Molson Ex and take in a segment of a man whose tattoo homage to a deceased pet goes horribly wrong. I order another drink, then another. I try to piece together a kind of mental scrapbook of my performances to date.

A young farmer comes in and sits alone with a beer. He looks over at me several times.

"I'm a musician," I say, not knowing how else to acknowledge his attention.

"Really." He looks satisfied.

The local news comes on. During a report about a recent drop in wheat prices, the farmer turns in his chair and says, "I play synth. Got the whole thing set up with the computer now. I can just make all this music! Great way to waste time. Specially now, after harvest."

"Yeah," I say.

"Is that a wig?" he asks, tentatively, then glances over at the other people in the bar, who are staring.

"No," I lie. "Yes—it's new."

"No problem."

We are silent for a moment.

"Ever recorded?" he asks.

"No, no. Just covers. Gigs."

"You here long?"

"I take off tomorrow. I have to get to the Alberta border."

"Well, you can come and see my set-up if you want. Farm's just up past the graveyard." He gets up from his table and stands over me. He makes me a map on the thin damp coaster that the waitress placed under my beer glass.

"Thanks," I say.

"Come out," he says, and walks to the bar to pay. The regulars are looking at him, then at me, and I wonder what they make of it. I get up a few minutes after he leaves and go outside with my map. I want to walk and think.

I follow the directions but get confused. Fifteen minutes later, I am still on the residential streets of the town and not anywhere close to a graveyard. I double back and realize I have to use the bathroom quite badly. I notice lights on and lots of cars parked around a grade school. I try the side door and find it's open. I walk down the green hall, which is lined with low coat racks and classroom doors, looking for the bathroom. The mixed scent of janitorial products and kids' belongings throws me back to my own childhood and to an image of my sister pulling down my shorts while I drink from a hall fountain.

Behind me, someone pops a head out from a door halfway down the hall. "Hey! Stacey! Hey!"

I turn and see a woman in heavy makeup, waving. "Come on. You're late. It's almost time."

Another woman comes out from the door dressed as a fisherman with a fake moustache, suspenders and wading boots. The two are gesturing for me to come over. I really need to go to the bathroom, but I turn and walk toward them.

"Who are *you*?" says the first woman, her forehead scrunched in annoyance, as I approach the door.

"I'm just here for the bathroom."

"Where's Stacey?" says the fisherman.

"I don't know who that is."

"Why do you have her wig then?" the first woman says.

I hesitate, put a hand up to touch the top of my head.

She looks upset. "The mermaid scene is next and the whole group's getting nervous. We've been calling Stacey for a half-hour. Jesus."

"Okay. Let's calm down a bit and think," says the fisherman, pressing the air with both palms. "Do you know the part?"

"Right! Like, you're not from town. Fine. But if you know the part, then all she had to do was call and tell us she was sending you. So? Do you know it?"

"No," I say, but regret it. I *do* know my part. "Yes."

The fisherman shifts her lips, considering, her drawn-on mustache going off-kilter. "So let's get a tail on you then."

They rush me in through the door, which opens onto a corridor. I hear singing, then a burst of applause. We are backstage. I'm not sure what to do next, but I can't turn back. We get to an area where other costumed adults stand—more fishermen, a whale, some sailors, and a man dressed as a lighthouse.

Everyone turns and sees me. Questions come into their eyes.

"No time for explanations," says the first woman from the hall. "Get the tail. She'll be the mermaid."

I have on the costume. My legs are not free to move much. A large swath of the iridescent green material swings out to the left of my ankles into the tail. On top, the costume is like a brassiere, with blue seashells sewn into the chest area of a skin-coloured bodysuit. Stacey must be smaller than me, because it's too tight across the back. I stand in the wings and think about the pressure exerted on the seams, wonder what I am doing. No one stands still long enough for me to ask. I can see the actors onstage. I can see a slice of audience through the mist of the stage lights.

Then, it's my turn. I know because the woman fisherman comes up and gives me a push. I am out onstage, walking in mini steps over to a big fake rock that must be meant for me.

I sit. A fisherman, this one played by a man, stands across the stage, beside his boat.

"The gods are toying with me!" he says excitedly, swinging an arm with dramatic flair up and in my general direction. "How else to explain that my eyes, *my hungering dry eyes*, this moment behold the greatest beauty there is?"

"Don't be fooled," says the boat, who is really a man in a

brown triangle of boat-shaped foam and tights. "She is but a mirage! You have been looking so long, you couldn't tell a mermaid from a Minotaur—anything real from the products of your starved stomach."

Two or three people in the audience chuckle.

"No!" says the fisherman, walking toward me in slow steps. The boat keeps pace with him. "You're wrong. And why am I talking to a boat anyway?" More chuckles.

"It is true, I am lonely. I have been at sea for such a long time that my eyes could play fools to any whim, but they do not do so now. Oh no! *This* . . . this vision before me is real. Real as my heart, anyway. Real as the love that grows in me like the storm that swept me to this terrible place so many moons ago. How could such beauty be trickery? Why, just listen! *Listen* to her sing!"

The actor pretends to leap from the boat.

"Doooon't!" cries the boat, his mouth, which is nearly lost in brown face makeup, stretching into a wide "O."

The fisherman pretends to swim over to the rock where I am sitting. He is looking at me hard, as though it is my turn.

"I say—just listen to her sing!" he says again, and everyone is silent.

Someone in the back of the gym coughs. Offstage, the woman from the hall gestures to me wildly. "Sing!" she mouths.

And so I do. I sing the song I know best, the song I sang at my sister's wedding. I try to imagine that I am the mermaid. That I am Joni. The real thing. No dream. That I am beautiful, looking at life from another side.

When I finish, the actors are silent. The fisherman is still on the ground, technically drowned, but actually staring up, confused. Offstage, the fisherman played by a woman looks angry. A woman in a blonde wig nearly identical to mine stands beside her with wide eyes—Stacey.

But the audience. The audience is clapping without any more irony or dismay than the rest of the play appears to call for. I stand, careful not to fall over my tail. I try not to focus on the way I bulge around the tops of the shells in my costume, or on nagging images from childhood, or on my next gig. The stage lights are so warm, my head sweats. I want to undress. In my jeans is the farmer's map. It will be easier to find him in the morning. I take a bow and exit, stage right.

THE WOMAN ON THE MOVE

AFTER KAFKA

The woman on the move believes in motion passionately and hears God in all moving things. The lowliest housefly struggling against a window. A swerving vehicle. Still, she never intended to end up moving all the time. She started out like many others, moving around with her family. Her father's job took them from city to city, neighbourhood to neighbourhood. In each place, the woman on the move, then just a girl, played probably more than average the game of running wherever she went, of hovering with ants in her pants, as her father put it. But such frequent relocations and rambunctiousness were just slight exaggerations of the normal.

It was one specific day that set her on the path towards her adult obsession. Her father had taken her to the mall, where they came across a statue performer dressed in silver body paint, touted as being able to hold her posture all day without adjusting even a muscle. The girl was awestruck, then gradually repulsed by the pleasure this woman provoked in the crowd just by being static. She tugged on her father's sleeve, demanding to leave for the toy store, the pet store—anywhere but there.

But her father was enchanted. He crouched beside his daughter and held her tightly in a gesture of love. To the child, with that terrible silver woman in sight, his embrace felt like prison. He was oblivious. He smiled as the performer maintained strict right angles at the elbows and a hard-as-metal stare. She reminded him, he told his daughter, of his own grandmother, who had retired to a farm at eighty and would sit on her porch, motionless, watching the days begin and end. He had loved his grandmother, who'd seemed more plant than human, like a safe tree he could climb.

At some point the girl managed to free herself. She fled into the mall, running up the escalator then around the food court, where she happened to look up into the glassed-in ceiling and notice the sun's rays breaking apart among the peaked windows. For an instant the girl leaned against a plastic table letting warmth play over her face, over her T-shirt and sneakers. Then she knew as surely as her heart beat that she would never be still again.

There were hurdles along the way. The girl surmounted them. She sought legal emancipation from her parents and won it. Her passion grew. At eighteen, she got serious, rigging up a system of pulleys that would raise each limb in succession so she could move during her sleep. She travelled continuously, using the night hours to double her geographic coverage. She thanked God (who, for her, from that day at the mall onward, was more sunbeam than human form) for giving her life at a time when constant motion was possible. Taking the money her parents had saved for her post-secondary education, she bought the most powerful palm-sized computer available and a satellite phone with world-wide reception. With these she made arrangements for planes, trains, mules, boogie boards—whatever the situation demanded. While travelling from Point A to Point B she paced. If for some reason she could not, she would swing her legs or even, in dire circumstances, twiddle her thumbs.

Soon, it became apparent that to pursue movement at this level, she needed help. While jogging in place in the square outside St. Peter's in Rome, the woman on the move had an inspiration: she dialed the number for her cousin and offered her a job. The cousin, an executive who travelled a lot, seemed like the perfect candidate, but she was reticent. She had a fiancé, had been thinking of settling down. The woman on the move wouldn't hear another word, insisted on an answer. She disparaged her cousin for being prematurely old, told her she was missing her chance to truly experience the world. The cousin, affected by this argument, accepted and was put in charge of sponsorship, public appearances, accommodations and transportation. She asked her fiancé for an indefinite time-out and told herself there'd be plenty of time to settle down later.

The woman on the move began appearing on television. News cameras showed up wherever she did. Always, they found her dressed in one of seven trademark jumpsuits, one for every day of the week, each a single bold colour from head to toe. She owned nothing more, having abandoned skirts and heels, pants and blouses as symbols of the tethered life. Besides, she despised bulk and saw her ultra-lean form as a living challenge to immobility, something to be flaunted. Sponsors, from athletic shoe companies to airlines, seeing that she had a hand in promoting an aspect of modern life in which they also held a stake, competed for every scrap of space on the zip-up one-pieces.

The woman on the move enjoyed all this attention and found it humourous to watch encumbered cameramen jog after her. The journalists all asked the same questions: Why move so much? What would be enough? Didn't she ever want a husband? Kids? The woman on the move answered their questions patiently, often repeating her mantra that "stillness is decay; to move is to improve."

Crowds, too, came to hear her speak. She charged no fee. Instead, she insisted that for the length of her presentations the audience move too. Those who could not due to age or disability were provided with wheelchairs, walkers, strollers—every aid to bring them up to speed. Those who still couldn't manage it or who refused were asked, politely, to leave. "On the move" imitators started popping up. Now there were malls where people were hired to wear jumpsuits and move constantly. The woman on the move felt a deep satisfaction at the thought of the statue performer she'd seen as a child forced to wash away her false metal, zip up and get going.

At a certain point, and while her cousin-manager tried to dissuade her, she decided to delve deeper into movement. She was no longer satisfied with passive motion during the night. She already had guards who watched her constantly—hired by the sponsors to verify that she never stopped moving. She asked these guards to wake her every half hour so that she could spend the other half doing something productive. This vastly increased her popularity, with people everywhere amazed at her unprecedented sacrifice to locomotion.

Their fascination, though, increasingly saddened the woman on the move. Some nights she might be outside doing sit-ups and find herself staring at the waxing or waning moon, wishing people could understand: she had no choice but to be the woman she'd become. She couldn't seem to communicate that there was no limit to her ability to move, that it was as easeful as breathing or the tides coming eternally in and out, tugged by the moon and sun. And she knew that she was the forebear of a much greater era, one when people would be rid of the chains of permanence. As time went on, perhaps due to a lack of REM sleep, the woman on the move became more detached and thinner, skin and sinew in the jumpsuits. The press regularly noted her resemblance to an aging pop star twenty years her senior. She cut back on her talks to preserve her strength, though people came just to watch her walk through airports or swim across admittedly narrower and narrower canals. They wanted to see the person who spent all her time on the go, shuffling, waving, hair-tossing, even bowing her life away, and they didn't mind that she was so pale or that she spoke in a diminished voice and said next to nothing.

The woman on the move also withdrew from the people closest to her. Her guards often changed, after all. Some had families and couldn't stay on the road indefinitely. Her relationship with her cousin became strained after the cousin began whispering with her ex-fiancé over the phone.

One day the woman on the move was walking backwards on one of the raised plains at Machu Picchu, followed by a group of South American journalists, occasionally whispering a word to her audience through a translator, when an emergency call arrived. "Princess," said a distant, crackly voice. It was her father. He had been experiencing bouts of senility and was confined to a room at a care facility. The woman on the move had not once visited him there. His voice sounded ghostly, reaching her from across the continent. "It's my time, Princess." The woman on the move was shaken. She abruptly wrapped up her public appearance. The journalists looked confused, but most smiled in admiration. They understood: she had places to be; you couldn't hold someone like her back.

Her cousin reminded her that they were scheduled to fly to Antarctica that night, where the woman on the move was due to address some scientists while crossing an icefield. The woman on the move paced along the edge of the plain, the thin oxygen of the Andes causing strange thoughts to enter her mind. She saw herself once more at that mall so many years before. But now, the scene unfolded from the perspective of the statue performer, and her eyes literally stung from the memory of the silver paint that had covered the woman to her very lashes. She felt her breathing slow and a disturbing sense of calm spread through her limbs, chilling the space between her skin and her jumpsuit. A moment later, she snapped herself out of it. She advised her cousin to cancel Antarctica and order an oxygen tank to the hotel room in Lima. She would reacclimatize before the next plane out.

On the flight north, the woman on the move did yoga and Tai Chi, refused food. She considered her decision. She had long resented her father for not accepting her way of life. She suspected that he'd absorbed the idea propagated by her critics: that if she had loved some one person more, perhaps him, perhaps another, she would have remained somewhere gladly, and that what had made her movement so easy was her empty heart, her moon-like indifference to people and places. The woman on the move knew this was nonsense—jealous, psychobabbly nonsense. She had to move. It was the time for movement, couldn't they see? And yet, her father was dying, and she understood that his own dwindling time also mattered, not for sentimental reasons, but because he was to undergo a great, forced movement from this life into whatever came next—perhaps a purer, light-like form of movement. Her heart rate quickened at the thought.

Her cousin prodded her about logistics: how would she continue moving while keeping a death vigil? A bedside exercise bike? A hospital room made mobile? There would be problems at the border.... They debated the entire way.

When the woman on the move finally arrived at the steps of the old age facility, it took all her determination not to freeze at what she saw. On the sprawling porch, which was shaded by oaks whose leaves drooped like tired, open palms in the hot afternoon, her father, who was dressed in a pale undershirt, shorts and flip-flops, who appeared to have been squeezed into the body of someone half his size, like he'd been put through the dryer, was pushing away two attendants as he tried to reach for his toes, then managed a single, demented-looking jumping jack.

The woman on the move ran up the steps. He's completely lost his mind, she thought. But when their eyes met, she knew: her father was using up his last spurt of energy to do as she had: he was embracing physical movement. He continued flailing, his stubbled cheeks blanched, the skin under his exposed arms swinging in puckered waves. Shooing away the worried attendants, the woman on the move watched as his eyes bulged with effort. Mid-motion, he extended his parched mouth up to her ear, his chapped lips almost grey, and whispered to the daughter he had never truly known, "I'll move with you from now on." And then he straightened from head to toe, slackened, and died.

She did not cry out. She didn't want the attendants to come running with their gurney, in their haste to ready her father for the grave. Instead, she looked to her side and noticed a wicker chair further along the porch that had an unimpeded view of a green slope and a far-off pond mirroring the bright sky. She lifted her father's diminished body into her arms and began to walk towards that chair. His thin hair was patchy, and one long section flopped over and was pulled down by gravity, covering an ear. His flip-flops swung from his stiffening toes. They made a perfect contrast: the limp father, and the woman on the move standing very tall, her bright jumpsuit covered in logos and symbols and flags.

She considered the moment of death. It had not been as she'd thought. It had not moved her. Worse, her father had only pledged motion for her sake, not his own. Now he was gone and the woman on the move felt certain that they had both deluded themselves, that there was nothing more to it. This knowledge filled her with unfamiliar, depleting sorrow. A valve seemed to open up inside her and conviction began to flow out and away. She envisioned depositing her father's corpse in the wicker chair, a fitting end, a return to his grandmother's vegetable-like state. She saw herself sprinting away, returning to her cousin and the rental car. She was only a day's travel from the limitless icefields. But nearing the chair, such weariness overtook her that she sat down with him still in her arms. She knew it wasn't from love, since she had never felt close to her father, and had certainly not cherished him as he had her. But what else, then? She looked out at the pond, resplendent with the sunlight shimmering over its glassy surface—stillness and movement somehow interrelated. For once, her mind did not hop to the next subject but remained puzzling over this momentary bind, as she remained seated in the chair, the full weight of her father's body laid across her lap, her lavish sneakers resting on the bare porch boards for so long she didn't notice herself losing time.

ACKNOWLEDGEMENTS

Like all stories, these have evolved. My fellow MFA students at UBC creative writing, as well as Linda Svendsen, Keith Maillard and Madeleine Thien reviewed first drafts. Later versions were published in *Taddle Creek, Grain, The New Orphic Review, Exile: The Literary Quarterly, The Dalhousie Review, Verandah,* and *subTerrain.* Thanks to the readers and editors at those journals, especially Conan Tobias and Brian Kaufman. My own readers are Nick Kazamia, Anar Ali and Adam Frank. Thanks also to Lynn Coady for support and advice. Grants from the Canada Council and BC Arts Council kept me going midway. Thank you to the board members at NeWest Press, for saying yes; to Matt Bowes, for his work in preparing the book; and to my editor, Anne Nothof, for her attention and patience. Finally, to my family— the big Pigeon one and this littler Frank/Pigeon one here on the coast—I'll gladly go wherever you take me.

Vancouver-based Marguerite Pigeon is a former journalist and traveller turned writer of fiction and poetry. Her work has appeared in *Grain*, *subTerrain*, and *The Dalhousie Review*. Her first poetry collection, *Inventory*, was published in 2010, while her novel *Open Pit* arrived from NeWest Press in 2013.